Gift from a
Fat Fairy

Eric Hodgson

To Nikki
With all my
love

Eric
xx

Colchester

Those of you who know Colchester will think I don't...
I was born and raised here. I've just had some fun:
solved the congestion problem with a fab mono rail;
moved Col U's ground from Suffolk, back into town;
situated Essex University in the Town Centre; added
some terrific riverside bars and cafés; and... some
streets you wouldn't really want in any town.

QR Code for Gift from a Fat Fairy on amazon.co.uk

Or... look for Gift from a Fat Fairy by Eric Hodgson
on any Amazon site

Gift from a Fat Fairy

The undercover cop took control. Shouting. "Who's hurt?"

"Dais is," I shouted back.

"No... I'm alright... I think." She had a shallow nick across the side of her forehead.

My heart was thumping. I should imagine everybody's heart was thumping. I double checked with Dais, she assured me that she wasn't badly hurt. She was clearly shocked. I sat her up, leaning against the wall, and stood.

The cop came over, grabbed my shoulder and pulled me to one side... "Well done... you did alright."

One guy and one girl dead... shot, and two guys badly hurt. Blood everywhere. Lots of crying. One of the girls, who said she had been to medical college, was trying to make the injured comfortable. The thug was dead. Eighteen of us left... me, the cop, seven guys and nine girls. We had the two Uzis. Down here, under the duck farm, was a maze; the cop instructed a group to search the rooms that were inter-connected to the room we were in... and to look for another way out.

"Are you okay?" he asked me.

I nodded.

"Thanks, you may have saved our necks."

I felt ten feet tall at that moment, but I hadn't been brave, I told him. It had been instinctive, trying to save Dais.

"Well, you saved her."

I looked over to Dais. She was still crying. Reese and Hanna were comforting her. Reese, ever the journalist, was probably looking for another story. As they talked, they all turned and looked in my direction...

"Any of you know how to use an Uzi?" asked the cop. A stupid question, except...

"Me," I answered. I was the only one.

The cop laughed a short laugh and tossed me the other gun. "Well, it's up to us then. How do you feel about going up those stairs and out of the front door?"

"Funny thing, I was thinking of doing just that."

"Come on then."

We edged through the door and crept up the stairs. He beckoned me to stand back before plunging into the big dirty room that was between us and the outside world. It was empty. I followed him. There were no windows, just a door, which he slowly pulled open. Blinding sunlight flooded in, but that was all... no bullets.

He waved his arm, beckoning. "Come on."

We stood with our backs to the wall, one each side of the door, Uzis at the ready, alternatively sneaking quick looks across the yard. The vehicles were still parked.

"It looks as though they're still around," he whispered.

Hanna had followed us up the stairs. From across the room she whispered, "Hey."

We looked around, she was holding up a mobile.

"We found it on the dead gangster."

"Brilliant... well done," said the cop, "we'll all get out of this, yet."

Screams and shouts from downstairs. The lights had gone out.

"The bastards have turned off the power. It must mean that they are going to attack!"

He turned to Hanna. "Go down and tell them all to keep calm, and quiet."

Hanna disappeared. We waited. Outside, just the continuous hum of quacking, everything else eerily still.

"How many of them out there, do you think?"

I assumed he hadn't meant ducks. Earlier, the cop had said there were ten thousand in each building... that meant one hundred thousand ducks. I thought back to when I was hiding between the sheds. "There are four Russians, Red Walton, the smarmy bastard who shot Dais, an' at least five Gilberts."

"Gilberts?"

"Gangsters. They all look like Gilbert."

"I haven't seen Gilbert lately."

He was right. If Gilbert wasn't here, it meant that we really did have a good chance of getting out of this alive. "No," I said, "come to think of it, nor have I." A quick peek. "I can't see his grey car."

He checked the mobile. No signal.

"I was in that shed, over there, I think." I tried to work out where the grey car had been parked. "I got a signal on the phone you gave me when I was half way along, inside it."

He punched in one-one-two.

"Don't forget, when I dialed that, crooked cops turned up."

He winced and stopped the call. After a couple of thoughtful seconds, "I know who to call, don't worry. I'll be able to get in contact with him via emergency services."

"Who yer gonna call? Dial his number now, then, if you get killed, I'll be able to get to the right person. I'm not trusting normal cops."

He looked at me long and hard. "Good thinking." He punched in some numbers. "Right, it's the last dialed number other that the one I'm going to make now."

After all that, the phone didn't work.

The disappointment with the mobile produced a careless moment… we both slipped our heads around the edge of the doorway at the same time… a mistake.

My face was stung. They had been waiting for the moment. Ratatat... ratatat. Dust, stones and splinters of wood erupted from around the front of the building and the noise was deafening as bullets smacked against the outside of the building. Two or three ricocheting actually around the room. I tried to pull back from the doorway but my jacket snagged and I saw them charge out from between the sheds opposite. I squeezed the trigger and they dived for cover. The cop immediately understood what was happening and leapt out from behind me, firing, making a dash for the Russian lorry, about twenty yards away. A Gilbert went down and the others turned and ran. The cop made it. "Yesss..." he shouted as he jumped up into the back of the truck. He was mad!

All was still again, but they were out there, waiting. Regrouping. I wondered, unbelievably for the first time, what it would be like, to die. I wanted to see Josh before I did, find out where he was. And it would be nice to see Fallon... and the gang.

Thinking didn't help. Thinking was making me scared.

Day 1 Thursday

Fallon was the only girl in the *castle gang*. She lived and grew up in our street and was an important cog and a tart. We'd all had her, over and over. She told me I was the best, which was sad because she meant nothing to me, I just used her.

We had been discussing a problem outside the chippie at lunch time, all the gang was there. A couple of other kids we owed favours to had asked us to get a teacher in the shit. If it was worked right it was quite easy to get one suspended, at least. We'd done it before. Mr Morgan! When he was wound up he would lose it and poke his finger in your face while he shouted at you. The plan was that Fallon would wind Morgan up so much that he'd shout and holler and poke his finger. She was to make out that he'd got her in the eye, hold her hands to her face, fall over, then jump up and run from the classroom. Stick would be waiting, out of sight around the corner, and he was to poke his finger hard into her eye, so it looked authentic. Fallon didn't fancy it.

It had been Mo's plan. He was pissed that she wouldn't go along.

"Let Stick poke you in the fuckin eye instead," she said.

"Morgan has to poke me first... he wouldn't, would he? He wouldn't poke any of us cos he'd be scared of getting a poke back."

"Well I ain't fuckin doin' it. It could destroy my looks for ever."

"Come on, what looks?"

"Fuck off."

"Can't we find someone else?" asked Franny.

"From the class? Who can we trust to go along with it, an' anyway, they're all too soft, like her?"

"Fuck off."

What about getting someone else to wind him up, pretend to get poked in the eye but don't tell her what Stick was going to do… That's what I was thinking, was mulling over and perfecting before opening my mouth. The idea was awesome!

"What about getting someone not in the gang to do it, to wind Morgan up an' pretend to get poked in the eye, just like we planned, but don't tell her that Stick's gonna do his bit to her." It was Lee! Fucking Lee. I couldn't believe it.

"Fuckin brilliant," said Mo.

I was so pissed. My idea and Lee gets all the credit!

The plan was adopted. Fallon was given the job of finding a collaborator/victim and everyone went back to school, going over and over 'fucking Lee's brill plan' and who the lucky 'to be poked in the eye' sucker might be. Everyone except me, that was. I was so pissed I slipped off and walked to the park.

Nothing ever seems to work in my favour... other than the time when Greenwood, our maths teacher, had a go at me at school.

I was changing classes, between lessons. "Boy. Get that hood down," he shouted.

Any other time and I'd have just slipped the top down, but walking along the corridor was Josh and his mates. Josh is my little eleven-year-old brother. I'm his big hero. Added to that, he's held in high esteem by his mates because his big brother (me) is part of the *castle gang*, and he was well within earshot when Greenwood hollered out his order.

Anyway, Greenwood really was a tosser, and I definitely wasn't afraid of him. "Fuck off." I sidestepped and slipped out through the exit.

According to Josh, Greenwood went ballistic and ran after me, but tripped before he reached the door... smashing his face on the floor. All the kids in the corridor were in stitches. He then made the fatal mistake of claiming one of them had tripped him. When they checked the CCTV, he was proved to be a liar. I never saw him back at school after that.

That was the best moment of my life. Every kid in the school knew it was me under that hood, but, hard as they tried, the teachers never found out. Suddenly I was well respected, not for being Mo's best mate, but for getting a teacher expelled.

Mo was my mate, probably still is. He's the hardest kid in school, and he's still fifteen. His granddad came from Pakistan and was a strict Muslim, but his dad had married a Sikh. All the Pakistani and Indian relations threw Mo's mum and dad out of the families. Mo's real name is Mohamed, but no-one calls him that, not even his mum. If you want to get beat up, call Mo Mohamed. I'm his mate because we grew up together, if we hadn't he'd probably have nothing to do with me. I had never actually been in a fight... not then, anyway.

I don't know how long it took for the word to get out that Greenwood was proved to be a liar, but as soon as it did, we all bunked off and celebrated. "Fuckin hell, you was brilliant," said Mo. All the others agreed with him, except maybe Stick. Stick hardly agrees with anybody, not even Mo.

Stick is the strangest one in the gang. He's average size: straight back, straight hair, straight arms and legs. Everything is neat, his face, the way he dresses. Straight and neat, except for his thoughts. Nobody knows what he's thinking, other than he's always looking to whack someone; "What you staring at..." and if the victim says the wrong thing, which is just about any combination of words you can think of, Stick will give him a hammering.

And when he laid into someone the rest of us watched, laughing. If the bloke had mates they generally kept well out of it, on account of it would be Mo and the *castle gang* they'd be taking on. That's not really me though. Oh, I laughed, outwardly, but I always felt sorry for the bloke who was getting a hiding. But I think I was the only one.

Being brutally honest, I think I'm the cleverest one in the gang. I always get the right answer, it just takes a while, and so when I do, the moment has gone and I never get the recognition I deserve. Even when I do know what to say, I worry that it might not be right, so, just in case, I say it under my breath.

I sit next to Mo at school. Because I'm quiet and he's not, even the teachers think I'm the thick one. I remember once we were given a test, history, and because she (Miss Crabtree) assumed it was me who always copied Mo, she made us sit apart. I got top marks! Mo didn't. I couldn't gloat, but…

I'm okay with Josh. Really, being truthful, I suppose my relationship with the gang had always been false, a sort of self-preservation. It was alright until the Greenwood incident, but after that I had an image to live up to as well… I found that hard work. The respect I commanded at school was undeserved, I'm a fake. Living a lie is alright in short bursts. I have that image burden thing with Josh as well, but our friendship is real… is, was? Although he's four years younger than me, he's braver, much braver. My image and his bravery are why I'm in this deep shit now.

Chapter 2

It sort of started with Greenwood, but this story is a mix of things happening, of people manipulating and people being manipulated. Rosie had spent a long time manipulating. It was like she'd been steadily preparing the main ingredient, me, then pushing *me* into position, standing back, passing me over to Greenwood to apply the finishing touch. Michael Deer lit the fuse. Rosie's our step mum. Our real mum left when I was six and Josh was two. I asked Dad once where she'd gone, "Fuck off and mind your own business." I never asked him again, you don't ask my dad tricky questions. I don't know what got into me that time.

But Rosie had definitely been a big factor in the way the story began. Rosie wasn't her real name, that's what Dad called her. I remember the first time, vividly, I was seven. I don't know why, but I wasn't at school. I don't know where Josh was because I was on my own, playing in the garden. I'd found a dead frog and was dissecting it. My hands were covered in slimy frog guts. She went ballistic, "Get that fuckin thing out the garden." But before I could, she hit me, and hit me… and hit me.

I tried to stop her by putting my hands up and soon I was covered all over with shitty slime, on my face, my jumper, my jeans, in my hair… I was a mess. Suddenly she stopped. She must have felt sorry because she pulled me against her and hugged me, and her anger disappeared as quickly as it came. She held me to her for a long time, until I stopped crying. Then she said, "What a mess!" By then she had got the stuff on her as well.

I was still snivelling when she took me upstairs and ran the bath…

She beat me lots over the next few years. I almost got to enjoy it, knowing what was going to follow… I was loved and cherished and felt wanted. Every now and then she'd whisper that I must stay home from school… I never told anybody; she said if I did I would end up thrown out onto the street and, more importantly, everybody would laugh and make fun of me. Anyway, she stopped by the time I went to Saint Hel's, when I would have been old enough to know what's right and what's wrong and too old to put up with that sort of behaviour.

I wondered about Josh and Rosie.

Chapter 3

Colchester's cool. It's got more homeless than London. Official. The University's situated in the centre of town and there's a load of fashion colleges. So, as I said, it's a pretty cool place to hang out. There are lots of shop jobs and bar jobs and it attracts a lot of people looking for work... too many. But that's okay, being such a mega shopping centre and tourist attraction means there's generally some way of getting cash, legally or otherwise, so, even if you're down on your luck, it's worth staying.

Trouble is, because of the homelessness, there's interference from unwanted sources. A local group of women called Boudicca's Angels are out to save people, young people. You can't walk through the park, especially on a school day, without the busy-bodies accosting you. If you're stupid enough to tell them you're bunking off, they won't leave you alone until they watch you walk back through those school gates.

This day was no different, and I wasn't in the mood to be accosted, so I found a place in the bushes overlooking the lower park.

And what I saw was interesting. The Angels stopped and spoke to everybody. They worked in two groups, four in one and five in the other, and it looked well co-ordinated. When they came across someone they thought they could help, all nine women crowded around like flies on a turd and did their stuff. In a period of just over an hour they led away three people, two girls and one bloke, probably to give them food and a new start in life. One of the girls went off with two blokes in a car, but at that time I didn't really think too much about it.

Michael Deer. Queer. He was intercepted. He's thirty, fat, sweaty and lives two streets from our house. His mum is one of the Angels. Now Michael Deer, queer, is someone not to be messed with; hard fucker, says Mo, never let him corner you. Yet watching him with the women made me want to puke, all luvy-duvy, arms waving, kisses thrown… It was rank.

I'd downloaded some great gear, and watching the Boudicca do-gooders and listening to that kept my mind off fucking Lee nicking my great idea.

I watched him come up from the bottom of the park. I saw it was him as he passed the boating lake: Josh. Why wasn't he in school?

There's a high Roman wall that cuts the bottom park in two, and from where I was I could see four Angels walking alongside it at precisely the right speed to intersect Josh as he passed through the gateway. They couldn't see him and he couldn't see them but both were on a collision course and there was nothing I could do to save him, I just watched, helpless.

I couldn't hear anything, obviously, because of the distance and 'Florence And The Machine', but there were plainly lots of questions and lots of bending over and conferring. Then there were some pats on Josh's shoulders and head, and loads of smiles. Josh walked on. I was amazed, what had he told them? How did he do it?

"Why aren't you at school?" we both said at the same time, I was laughing a bit, he wasn't. I must admit he'd looked pretty miserable as he approached. I'd collared him as he reached the top of the park.

I pulled him into the bushes, "Why?" I asked again.

He shrugged. "Couldn't be bothered to go back."

"Go back?"

"Yeah, go back."

Somehow that felt good to hear.

"After lunch," he continued.

"Oh, right."

"Why?"

"I dunno, curious."

He kicked at the ground. He seemed guilty about something.

"After lunch you say."

"Yeah."

"Where're you going now?"

21

"Town."

"What for?"

"Rosie's got a toothache an' I'm going to pick up a prescription from the dentist."

The mention of Rosie stirred up some feelings. "So you went into school this morning?"

"Yeah."

Josh wasn't acting normal. He looked as though he was about to burst into tears. "Okay. Do you want me to come with you?"

"No, it's okay."

"Oh. Alright. Seeya later then."

"Yeah seeya," he turned and left. Something wasn't right, he was acting weird.

I went back to the house at four, after school had packed up, so Rosie wouldn't know about me bunking off. That didn't work, she'd been sent a text from school.

"Didn't go back to school this afternoon then?" That's all she said, which I thought was a bit sussy, not mentioning Josh being off as well.

I kept my eye on them both all evening, to try and see if I could read into anything from the way they acted, but, apart from the shitty mood Josh was in, there didn't seem anything untoward. The next morning I asked his form teacher if he'd been at school yesterday morning, but the cow wouldn't tell me, so I had to pull one of his mates aside, who said he'd been absent all day. "Don't tell Josh I've spoken to you," I said.

"He ain't here today either."

This was serious.

Chapter 4

Day 2 Friday

I needed to satisfy myself that Rosie wasn't up to her old tricks, with Josh instead of me, and decided to skip maths and slip home and check things out. Getting out of the school isn't easy during lesson time, but I was presented with a stroke of luck you couldn't have planned. A bull appeared on the football pitch! I'm not kidding, where it had come from, I don't know. I was tempted to stay, see if it mauled anyone to death, and I had to make a tough decision… still, it had presented me with the opportunity I needed, so while eyes were trained in the opposite direction I slipped through the gate.

I was getting more and more nervous as I got closer to the house. I quietly slipped my key into the lock, pushed the door and crept in, all the time with my ears and eyes alert and all the time half expecting to be smashed around the head as I poked it into each room. A strange feeling crept through my body, not an unpleasant one!

The whole house was quiet and empty. The last place I checked was the bathroom. Nothing.

So, I asked myself, what was Josh up to? leaning back on the hand basin... Perhaps Rosie had taken him out... I soon discounted that though: just too weird, too unlikely.

Anyway, they weren't in. The unlikelihood that a teacher might at that very instant be having his intestines stretched out all over the football pitch by the horns of a raging bull meant there was no reason for me wanting to return to school. It would have been a waste of life to go back, so I decided, as it was Friday, to wind down and begin my weekend early. I ran a bath and threw off the uniform.

I relaxed in the bath, thinking about Rosie and Josh, together. That got me thinking about me and Rosie, in the old days. Instead of getting angry, it started to get me aroused. I had to stop myself, it wasn't right. I switched my thoughts to Fallon, to take my mind off Rosie. I imagined us together... In my mind, I imagined running my hands up Fallon's naked legs, which I always liked doing, starting at her ankles. Slowly... she's got nice smooth pins. Higher and higher I went. I looked up... it wasn't Fallon looking down, licking her lips seductively, it was Rosie. And it fucking was! She was in the bathroom... looking at me, at my... I was so surprised I reacted by having a massive, violent spasm and in one single jerk there was as much water over the floor as there was in the bath.

"Not at school again."

And I was totally at a loss for words.

"If you're gonna play with yourself you should lock the door," and she turned and left.

I was stunned, in a state of shock, and, I can assure you, no longer aroused. How did she get in without me hearing her? I'm sure my face must have been as red as a Man U shirt. God. I sunk my head below the surface of the water… The lock! I should lock the door. I reached out, my hand even touched it, I tried to slide it across. But it was no good, I couldn't bring myself to lock the evil woman out… I slumped back into the water… and waited.

And waited. The water was stone cold and my skin looked as though I'd borrowed it from some old granddad before I came to the conclusion that she wasn't coming back, and by the time I'd dried and dressed, the rest of the house was empty again.

Getting through the park unscathed was like being an escaped prisoner in the war, dodging the Germans. The Boudicca Nazis were out in force. England was the little clump of bushes where I'd hidden yesterday. There were a couple of close shaves but, after some cute manoeuvres, I made it. They didn't take anyone away while I watched, and before I knew it kids from the various schools and colleges began to spew out onto the grassy hillside to lie around for a sunny lunch break. The patrols disappeared.

Right through until the afternoon there was no sign of Josh. He didn't have a mobile because he kept losing them and they wouldn't give him anymore. If I was him, skiving off, I'd have used the cover of all these kids to get back and forth, that's why I'd chosen this place to look out for him.

By two o'clock the hillside was almost empty. All the kids had gone, just a few older people relaxing, and soon the Boudicca squads were back. And would you believe it, Josh waltzed right through them, hiya, waved, and walked straight past, without a care in the world.

"What did you fuckin tell em this time?"

"We have an understanding."

"What does that mean?"

Josh shrugged. His mind was obviously elsewhere. "Look at the fat dick ed."

"Don't change the subject."

"No, look. I wonder what it's like, being a poof."

I looked. Michael Deer, queer, was waddling through the bottom gate. "I dunno. I've never thought about it." And I hadn't. "It would be a waste of brain power."

"Kissing another bloke!"

We both pulled faces of disgust.

"Touching another blokes…"

"For fuck sake Josh."

"Well, that's what he does."

27

Did I think like this when I was eleven? He suddenly jumped up and ran down the back path from where our clump was, through the flowerbeds and out onto the main path behind the guy, and began to walk like a spastic Charlie Chaplin; mimicking the fatso's walk. Fuck! I tried to wave Josh away. "Don't do it," I mouthed, but to no avail.

He was funny though. Michael Deer, queer, suspected there was a piss-take occurring, but every time he turned around Josh switched to a slouchy schoolboy walk… even that was funny. The intelligent side of my brain told me to stop him, warn him… this geezer's not to be messed with, but my thick side sent laughing signals to my mouth, and it being the dominant force, I laughed and laughed until I couldn't see for laughing.

Soon Deer was close to our clump and could hear me. He stopped, and while he was breathing heavily and sweating like a pig, he was also mad with rage. "You little bastard, I fucking know you, Jerry's oldest. Come here you little…"

Well, although the thick half of my brain is the dominant bit, it wasn't that dominant, and no way was I going to him. I wanted to shout 'fuck off' all manly like, but it came out like a little mouse squeak, heard by no one. He began to climb the small slope towards me, grabbing at the taller shrubs and flowers, trying to pull himself up… that was a laugh.

"Leave him alone you fat poof, you homo, you're gonna have a heart attack fatso," shouted Josh.

Deer turned and lumbered back down to the path again, waving his arms in fury at my brother, who ducked and weaved at about half a mile an hour. "And I fucking know you!"

"Who am I then? What's my name?"

"I know."

"No you don't fatso. Queer… faggot... homo."

"I'll find out!"

Josh side stepped in slow motion as Deer made desperate lunges, and a complete fool of himself, in front of a few onlookers who had begun to gather.

"Leave him alone, he's just a kid," one shouted.

The look! I thought Deer was going to explode. Then, whatever he was about to do or say, he thought the better of it, turned, and walked away. Josh began to throw more insults after the retreating slob, but the onlookers quieted him down.

When everyone had drifted away, and me and Josh were alone again, we recalled every second of what had just occurred, even my squeaky fuck off. And we laughed and laughed so much tears rolled down our faces. We both did 'the walk' together. It was a real quality moment.

"Hang around here, I'll be about an hour." Josh suddenly said, and before I could react he was gone.

Well, I waited, for longer than an hour, but he didn't return, and I needed a crap.

Chapter 5

The toilets I chose were the ones by the monument, at the entrance to the top of the park. They were like any other thousand-year-old bogs... there would be as much illumination with the lights turned off. The outside was covered with ivy, including the small windows, and most of what lighting there was streaked through the open doorway. Anyway, I was washing my hands when the whole place suddenly plunged into darkness as the entrance was blocked... and blocking it was Michael Deer, queer!

Shit!

Michael Deer, queer, someone not to be messed with; hard fucker, says Mo, never let him corner you.

I wanted to plead with him, explain that it wasn't me who was taking the piss, say sorry that I laughed. Instead I just cried.

"Well, well, well." He was different, no longer the out of breath and ready to keel over. He had the look of a conqueror.

I turned my back to him. If he was going to belt me, I didn't want to see it coming. The mirror was just a dull shiny metal of some sort and you could hardly see any reflection, but I closed my eyes anyway.

I felt his presence as he closed in on me. I waited, holding my breath. Surely one thump and he'd knock me unconscious. I willed him to get it over with.

But no! He wanted to taunt me. This was his moment. I felt his breath on my neck, and then he stroked it. I wanted to scream… but I was one of the gang! If he'd hit me right at that moment, I'd have shattered into a thousand pieces.

He stood behind me, engulfing me, wedging me against the hand wash basin. He was more than a full head taller and his biceps were bigger than the neck he gently stroked. I thought I was going to faint… my skin felt weird, it tickled. Then I realised that his hands were under my shirt, caressing my body. I was so scared. While waiting for the blow that was surely about to end my miserable little life I didn't comprehend what was happening, not until one of his hands slipped down inside my jeans.

Even then, when I realised what he was doing… it still didn't register what was to follow.

When you are panicking, waiting to die, confused, there's just about enough of a functioning brain to work out what's happening with your cock. You don't notice anything more. You don't feel your jeans fall around your ankles. And by the time you register the pain, it's too late, you're being fucked. The only thing I can clearly remember, vividly remember, was… I was erect. I had a hard-on! This couldn't be happening. He was whispering whispers but I'll never remember what he said, other than… Yesss!! And at the same moment… *I* ejaculated into *his* hand!

I can't remember him leaving, just that I'd been left on the cold concrete floor. I pulled myself and my jeans into the closest cubicle and passed out. I used my pants to clean myself. My arse throbbed and I needed to rest, so I switched off my mobile and curled up against the pan.

All I could think of was coming into his hand, how it felt. No thoughts of revenge, not even shame, just that. All the rest came later. Eventually I sneaked back home, told Rosie I was ill, and went to bed, but not to sleep.

I went over it, over and over and over it again. I thought about the times I'd been with Fallon, and how I reminisced about my encounters with Rosie, and thought… I can't be gay. Please God… please don't let me be gay.

Eventually my thoughts turned to revenge. I needed to kill Michael Deer, queer, before he told anybody else what he'd done, before he told anybody about my…

I was thinking well enough to realise that it was unlikely that he'd boast about what he'd done, after all, I was still fifteen and he'd raped me… he'd go inside. But *he* would know, every time I saw him he'd be able to smirk. Perhaps I should go to the police. "*He forced me, raped me.*"

"*He wanted it, enjoyed it... got a hard on...*"

I had to kill him.

Faces appeared from below. "What's happening?"

I told them. Outside was a dead thug and an Uzi. We could do with that gun.

They told me that they'd found another exit! "What shall we do?"

They were asking me!

The cop was shouting. "They've gone, get the gun. "I'll cover you."

"Cover me," said one of the guys.

I moved away from the door and three of them made a dash, but before they got more than a couple of yards, firing started again. I tried to fire back, but the gun didn't work, I must have run out of ammo. Two didn't make it back. The Uzi was still out there. Seeing the bloody bodies, I suddenly couldn't move.

While there was no shooting, the cop kept trying to get me to crawl across to the yard and get the gun. I would have, if I could've moved, but I was scared. He kept swearing at me... I think I disappointed him. He gave up and turned his back to me.

Shouts and a burst of machine gun fire, followed by a short lull, then gunfire from a doorway from my left.

Some of our guys, girls as well, charged into the yard, waving an Uzi above their heads. They must have crept out of the exit I'd just learnt about and managed to overcome a Russian or a Gilbert. The undercover cop was laughing and spraying the far side buildings with a layer of bullets as he encouraged everybody… he really was crazy! The others made it safely to a pile of pallets. They had full view of the area in front of the lorry. The cop was in the back of it, with a good view of most of the buildings on both sides, but I think I was the only one who could see what was going on the right-hand edge… and that's where I saw Red Walton and two others crouched, waiting to attack.

Suddenly the whole of our side of the yard seemed to come alive. The noise was deafening as dirt and dust, splinters of wood and stones and bullets whizzed and whined through the air in all directions. I saw Red and his two blokes rush forward under the cover of the fire, unseen by the cop. Without a thought I jumped up and shouted a warning. The cop turned and opened fire. I saw Red and the other two go down. I had saved him!

Chapter 6

Day 3 Saturday

I must have slept, eventually, because the sound of shouting woke me. After a couple of attempts to drown out the noise by sticking my head under the pillow, I got up, dressed, and grabbed the two things I always make sure I have with me; the mobile and some cash. I checked on Josh. His room was empty. It didn't look as though the bed had been slept in.

I heard men talking and Rosie swearing as I rolled down the stairs. When I reached the bottom the lounge door opened and Dad poked his head out, "Scat!"

"But…"

"Scat, you heard."

"Where's Josh?"

"Jesus…"

So I scatted.

Parked outside the house was a cop car. That must have been the law I heard in the house. I was tempted to sneak back and find out what was going on, but common sense got the better of me.

It wasn't even nine o'clock, so there was no point checking out the gang. I decided to go and see Gantsy, one of Josh's mates who lived local. Strange? he hadn't seen Josh for days. Time to think…

Both the Central and the Marks Tey lines of Colchester's mono-rail run through Middleborough. A ticket lasts all day. I hopped on the Central and headed south. Normally I'd have passed the time by gaming on the mobile, but my mind was mostly full of being gay, part full of being raped and part full of Josh.

As the car ran through the bus station, East Gates, Greenstead, Wivenhoe Park and Wivenhoe I ran my eyes over various blokes, were they good looking? Did I fancy any? Did any of them turn me on? The fact was, none of them did anything for me. As a real test, at Wivenhoe, I imagined one bloke naked, and then imagined a girl the same way. I ran an imaginary hand over the bare back of first the bloke and then the girl. Without a lie, the naked girl did a lot more for me than the naked bloke, although, scary-scary, the naked flesh of the bloke was okay, until I realised that my imaginary naked bloke had the smooth skin of a girl's. As soon as I replaced it with hairy, spotty, lumpy stuff I was suitably repelled.

Although I passed that test, there was still the fact that one bit of me had reacted out of order yesterday, and, as they say; your cock doesn't lie! That thought was the truth and it made me feel sick inside. And then there was Josh… where was he?

That was the moment, *the* moment! That's when I realised what had happened. I wanted to puke.

Josh had seen it all… He'd come into the toilets to save me, because that's what he would have done, and saw me. Me! Me and my fucking stiff dick!

How would I have reacted had it been the other way around? I'd have been disgusted and never want anything to do with my brother again.

Josh hates me! He's run away because of what he saw. Homeless, because of his gay brother. Worst thing of all, he wouldn't have known I was being forced. It all made sense.

I pulled back from the window as the mono crossed the river into Rowhedge. I got off at the station and went and sat at the river bank. Rowhedge is supposed to be an old fishing village, but it seemed big and crowded to me, especially as I wanted to be alone. Everyone stared. "Fuck off, ain't you seen anybody cry before," it was embarrassing. Even the ducks kept hanging around, to take a look.

I walked for a while through the narrow streets, trying to clear my head, but all I could think about was how everybody was going to react when they heard the news. If I'd been any good at football, being gay would definitely have ruined a promising career. The only consolation was that my future as a pop star can only have been enhanced. Fuck. Who was I kidding? I couldn't sing.

Over the back of Rowhedge, it's brilliant. Sand pits. I'd never been there before and it looked a mega place to hang out. I decided to make a point of going there with Josh...

I felt like throwing myself into the river and ending it all, but, one: I could swim, and two: the tide was going out and there was a lot of mud to squelch through before reaching the water. Anyway, before I killed myself, I had to get some revenge. That fat bastard wasn't going to get away with what he'd done.

I didn't see them while I was waiting for the mono car. They were like identical twins, except there were two or three years difference in their ages, and one was bigger than the other. Okay, they weren't identical but, if the younger one was a couple of years older you definitely wouldn't have been able to tell them apart. They were beautiful.

Like I said, I didn't clock them until I was sitting on the mono. Unfortunately, they didn't clock me, period. Or that's what I thought. They had long dark blond hair and nice figures and sat about ten rows ahead of me, I couldn't take my eyes off them. I'd never felt like this about anybody before... and now two came along at the same time.

They got off at Wivenhoe Park. As they walked past my window the smallest gave me the most fantastic smile. My heart melted. All the way to Middleborough, I forgot about being gay and instead was devastated and broken hearted that I might never see the two again. I decided then that I'd ride the Central Line every day until I found them, and that when I did I would pluck up the courage to ask them who they were. I think I was in love and I soon started to plan how I could move to Rowhedge or Wivenhoe and start a new life with the two sisters, because that's what they were, they had to be, and leave this gay life behind me.

Chapter 7

From Middleborough I went back to the house. I didn't go inside. Just like every other Saturday around this time, Dad would be inside with his pissed mates, drinking themselves into a blind stupor, and I didn't fancy facing them. It was always the same; after a bout of being pulled around and teased, I'd get fed up, and leave. What was the point? I'd save myself the bother, although I needed to find out about Josh. The police car had gone.

Josh generally avoided the house at weekends for the same reason. I decided to try the park, our clump, although that brought back ugly memories.

As I approached I could see somebody lying on the ground, it was weird. Whoever it was, he was moving strange like, twitching really quickly, spasms, like he was having a fit. I crept closer, and when I was almost on top of him I realised that it was Stick! Without thinking I rushed forward and grabbed him. "Stick, Stick, are you okay?"

He jumped up so fast he sent me flying. "What the fuck?" He pulled back a fist. He was about to belt me.

I was on my back. I thought my time had come, "Stick… it's me. Stick, what's the matter?"

"What do ya think you was doin man?"

"I thought you were having a fit."

"A fuckin fit. Stick don't ave fits. Can't even listen to music in peace without some fucker jumpin on top of me. Good job it's you. Even you were *that* close to gettin it…" he held up a finger and thumb to indicate just how close… and he loudly sucked air through clenched teeth as he thought of what might have been.

Now I could hear it. Weird fast music, coming out of the ear piece that lay on the ground. The sound was tinny. I couldn't make out what it was. "What's that?"

"The Prodigy."

"The Prodigy?" I turned my nose up without thinking.

"Yeah, the fuckin Prodigy. What's wrong with that?"

I realised my mistake. "Nothing wrong with the Prodigy Stick. I was just surprised that you liked em, never heard you say so before." The Prodigy? They're the sort of shit my dad likes.

"You like em as well then?"

"Yeah. Everyone likes the Prodigy."

"No they fuckin don't."

"I thought they did."

"Well they fuckin don't. That's why I like em, cos no one else does."

"Well I like em."

"What's your favourite track?"

"Pandemonium." There was silence. I thought I'd got it wrong. Where the hell had 'Pandemonium' come from? I knew nothing about the Prodigy. The word was genuinely plucked from thin air.

He nodded thoughtfully as he acknowledged my incredibly good taste in music. "I like 'Breath', but they're all fuckin good ain't they."

"Yeah." I had to change the subject quickly, as he'd definitely see through my lie if we continued on the Prodigy. I could see he wanted to (stay on the subject), either because he'd finally connected with me after searching for a common interest for years, or he wanted to suss me out so he could kill me.

"You seen Josh?"

He pulled a face and shook his head, "Who's Josh?"

"My brother."

He sighed and held out his hands in despair. I was a time waster. "Why the fuck would *I* see *your* brother?"

Good question. "Stick, you have to help me. I think my brother has run away."

"Why should I fuckin help? He's your brother."

"Cos…" Shit, I couldn't burst into tears in front of Stick, of all people, but before I could have any sort of reaction he suddenly sort of stood upright, as if to attention.

"Your brother… Josh." And then he seemed to laugh a little. He hid his mouth with a hand. "Yeah, Josh. Shit it must be Josh. The word's out that a kid… some kid's been taken."

"Taken?"

"Yeah… taken… by the law."

"The law?"

"Yeah."

"The law, what d'you mean, taken by the law?"

"Well, fuckin arrested, that's what I mean."

"Arrested?"

"Yeah… arrested."

"Why?"

"I don't fuckin know, do I."

"But you must know, why say it if you don't know?"

"You fuckin doubting me. Read my lips… I don't know why!"

"Right. But he's been arrested?"

He nodded, looking real concerned.

His eyes followed me as I walked in a circle, thinking. "Arrested," I said under my breath. It couldn't have been this morning, I'm sure they wouldn't have made him make his bed before frog marching him off. It must have been last night. Why? "And you say you don't know?" I said without thinking. I looked towards Stick, waiting for a response, but he was back on the ground and plugged in. He was obviously restraining his movements, but his right leg was already twitching.

I was about to slip away when there was a crunching of branches under heavy foot. Michael Deer, queer, appeared out of nowhere, smiling a sickly smile. I backed off in horror.

"STICK!"

Stick jumped up. Deer stopped dead in his tracks. I knew Stick was hard, but up until this moment I thought his reputation stopped with the kids.

Deer's mouth opened and closed but nothing came out. He was petrified!

"What you want you fuckin poof?" And I saw a knife slip out of Stick's pocket.

Deer backed off at roughly the same speed as Stick moved towards him.

Stick's speed increased. As the fatso tried to move back faster, he stumbled. In a flash Stick was at him, his blade pressing against the flabby throat.

"I told you before what would happen if you ever came near me again."

I could see the terror in Deer's eyes. Kill him, I willed under my breath, slit his fat throat, *before he tells what he did to me*.

"No… please. I didn't know you was here," and he began to cry.

Do it stick… do it.

I watched as Stick slowly increased the pressure of the blade onto the neck. The skin was white where it met with the steel.

And then I realised what I was willing Stick to do… "Don't, Stick… stop, it'll be murder."

I saw the relief on Deer's face as Stick turned to look at me. I'll give the fat bloke credit where it's due. His hand moved faster than lightning and grabbed Stick by the wrist, forcing the knife away. They both tussled for a bit and the weapon flew to the ground. Deer pushed and made a dash for it… I thought Stick was going to follow… but he let him go.

We both watched as the fat fucker ran all the way down to the bottom of the park and out of sight without once stopping for breath.

"Was you gonna do him?"

"What do you think? Fuck. If you're gonna hang around with me, stay out of my face."

"You don't like the bloke then?"

The look told me to back off.

Suddenly Stick picked up his knife and his mobile and started to walk away. "Can't even listen to music in peace." He kicked at thin air as he went.

Common sense told me to let him go. Arrested? Before that last little episode I had been wondering if Josh had seen Deer attack me and had got him afterwards, but obviously *that* wasn't the case.

He still might have seen us though.

The wait was impossible. One of the guys had raised his head from behind the wooden pallets, machine-gun fire had nearly taken it off. Twenty minutes now, without incident, everybody too afraid to move. Six dead bodies littered the yard, a reminder of what was at stake. Two of ours, four of theirs.

I was scared… but that wasn't the reason. I needed to move, to see Dais. I needed to do something, other than just wait… and to be shot.

I slipped back into the room and down the stairs. Into the semi-darkness. There were still around eight or nine guys, including Dais and Reese, and the two badly hurt. I think Dais smiled as I approached, glad to see me.

"What's going on?" asked Reese, quietly. "Are they still there?" She shied away from the Uzi. I didn't let them know that it was useless.

"I think so… unless they've left on foot."

"There was more shooting… has anyone been… is everybody okay?"

"Yeah. Everybody's fine," I lied, "just hemmed in."

"And you're alright?" whispered Dais.

I smiled.

One guy, who I didn't know, asked, "The others, they went out the back, did they get away?"

I shook my head. "They're alright though, but they can't move. The bastards have them covered. Red's dead, or down, at least. An' at least five or six of his thugs. I think the ones left are mostly Russians, have to be. My eyes were becoming accustomed to the low light. "Where's Hanna?"

"She's guarding the back, the other way out… just in case," said Reese. "She's going to shout a warning if they try to come in that way."

I wondered why they hadn't tried. "I'm gonna see if we can escape that way. I'll come back for you, if it's safe."

Dais held out her hand and gently touched me.

"Emma's okay," I said.

She smiled and slipped the St Christopher necklace over her head. "Take this."

"I can't, it's your lucky charm."

"I don't need it, I've got you."

"But."

"Take it… please."

I squeezed her hand tightly as I took it. "Thanks. Don't worry, I promise I'll get us out of here."

Reese told me about the back way out. through one of the furthest rooms along the corridor, and then through a big fridge door.

It wasn't a long corridor. Dark, but not so dark I couldn't see, once I got used to it, and I soon found the fridge. Actually, it wasn't a fridge, just looked like one. The door opened, then I had to push a wall with shelves on. Behind that, a flight of stairs… clever bastards. Hanna was nowhere to be seen.

I figured that if I could get around behind the sheds that Red Walton had attacked, I would be able to see what the Russians were doing, that's where the last lot of machine gun fire had come from. All clear… I made a run for it…

Chapter 8

I didn't know what to do. Phone the gang? I didn't feel like it, and I couldn't go home! I didn't fancy hanging around the park either, with Deer on the loose… while it didn't look as though he'd be coming back for a while, you never knew. I decided to walk to Cowdray Avenue, to the U's football ground. I had a pass into the stadium because I had a job there during the season. I was always allowed in, even now, in the close season. The grounds-man, Bob, let me help him sometimes.

He was alright was Old Bob. He wasn't that old really, about the same age as my dad, but everybody knew him as Old Bob. There was another Bob, Mr Bob, one of the directors, so I suppose when they said things like 'Old Bob is taking a shit', you knew which Bob they meant.

As soon as I arrived I went and sat in the East stand, about half way up. Old Bob was certainly there, on the pitch. He was being interviewed by Mattie Wilson, ex Ipswich player and now television sports pundit. Weird! The guy holding the camera swung it in my direction, which I was used to, because of my years as a ball-boy I was often on the telly. I wondered if Wilson was going to climb the stand and interview me?

You could imagine it…

Hello sir, Mat Wilson, BBC. Can you tell me anything about the new high speed pitch that Colchester United grounds-man, Old Bob Bowers, has invented?

Only that every footballer who has ever played on it says it's the fastest and truest they've ever played on.

Are you an expert?

I'm a member of the castle gang.

The castle gang… from Saint Hel's?

Is there another one?

Well. In that case, did you see the escaped bull maul the headmaster yesterday? They say he was carried around the school playing field ten times with a horn up his bum. By the time the beast had finished with the poor guy, his guts were stretched the full length of the football pitch and into the girl's toilets.

No. I missed that, had much more important things going on… and they required my attention.

Wow, more important…

By this time the guy with the camera had stopped filming, and him and Wilson were just standing and having a normal conversation with Old Bob, who caught my eye. It looked like he beckoned me down. I wanted to go, but in case I misread him I smiled and nodded... but stayed put. The three walked off.

I felt strange, my stomach, I felt sick. "Maybe I'm pregnant," I joked to myself, but all that did was bring back the horrors of the day before... as if those memories needed any prompting. Once more my thoughts were tugged towards suicide, and that made me hate the fat bastard again. I shouldn't have stopped Stick, why should I be the one who has to die?

I sat for a long time, looking at the football pitch that had been my stage for many fantasies. For as long as can remember I've had bad dreams and because of them I've always found it hard to get to sleep. That's where the football fantasies came in; dreaming of scoring a wonder goal but always falling asleep before the adulation. It wasn't always football. I tried lots of things. One was girls, but that didn't work.

When I was little I was a US soldier, in the cavalry, riding high on my horse, on the lookout for red-skins always sent me to sleep. I never rode into battle. I saw them, *the injuns*, but I never stayed awake long enough to shoot one. But I grew out of that fantasy. And the one being a rampaging Viking, riding the helm of a long-boat, the rocking...

No. Now I dreamed of being the best footballer in the world, even at fifteen. The arguments when the fucking bastard of a headmaster tried to stop me playing for England and therefore becoming the youngest player ever to represent my country. I perfected every shot in my dreams... I was that professional; not content to practice and train only while I was awake…

Old Bob woke me. "A boy your age shouldn't be sleeping."

"Wasn't asleep."

He sat down beside me. "You see Mattie Wilson smash that ball into the net from the halfway line?"

"Yeah…"

He shook his head. "No you didn't, there's not even any goal-posts up."

"Oh. I thought you were talking about Ipswich versus Newcastle a few years back, when he scored the best goal of his career."

He just looked at me. I had him. I could see him trying to remember it. But he never would, because it never happened, I'd made it up. I felt a little moment of triumph when he confessed that his recollection of great goals wasn't as good as mine.

"Why didn't you come down and join us?"

I didn't answer.

"It's a shame. They're doing a bit about the U's, all that goes on behind the scenes during the close season. You could have been in it."

He had the perfect job, getting to meet all the players and probably not having to write anything, ever.

"How did you end in this job?" I asked him.

"End up?"

"Well. How did you get it? You don't even like football."

"It's not much of a story. Getting a job on the ground staff was the only job I could get after leaving school, and then they sent me to agricultural college. Now, what I don't know about grass…"

Old Bob seemed to go into himself and was quiet for a long while. Then he asked, "What about you? What are you going to do when you leave school? You can't sell hot dogs for the rest of your life."

"I don't sell hot dogs."

"I know, but I heard they were going to promote you next season. Have you given it any thought?

"What, about selling hot dogs?"

"A job… after leaving school, what are you going to do?"

"Don't know."

"Really?"

"Really."

"What are you good at, at school?"

"Don't know."

"That's stupid. You must know if you're good at something or not."

"It's not stupid… I don't like anything at school, so I don't bother. But if I did like something, an' I did bother, I might be good at it, so I don't know."

"Do you know anything about grass?"

"Me an' my brother are working on a secret high speed pitch for the government."

He laughed. "What, a kind of fast growing strain?"

"No, the kind that if you ran on it you'd run faster using no more effort than normal. The government want it for our sprinters in Team GB."

"You could be a bloody comedian."

After that we went to his shed and he made us both a mug of tea. But he'd got me thinking, what was I going do after leaving school? And where would I live? I couldn't see myself being with Dad and Rosie for much longer. All of a sudden there seemed a lot to life: Am I gay? What about my new life with the Wivenhoe sisters? Where's Josh? Will I kill queer Deer?

"Bob. My brother's gone missing."

"Missing?"

"Yeah, missing. Stick says he's been arrested."

"You should keep clear of that one, he's trouble."

"Well, maybe. But he says Josh has been arrested."

"Write your surname on this piece of paper and I'll make a few enquiries."

After about twenty minutes on the phone he told me that Josh wasn't at the police station, never had been. So, Stick *had* lied.

I liked Old Bob. This was the first time in my life that I'd spent serious time with an older person, exchanging normal words. All the others just handed out orders, putting me in my place. They were either paid to mix with me or had a responsibility for me, like my dad.

"Are you married?"

"No."

"Why not?"

"Because I'm not, no real reason, other than I've never met the right person."

Are you gay? I wanted to ask.

"I'm not gay, if that's what you were thinking."

"Nor am I."

"Good. That's okay then."

That was as close to sex as we got. The rest of the time was spent with him telling me what it was like being an adult and me telling him what it was like being a kid, and for the first time in my life I began to look forward to getting older. I think, by the look on his face at times, he was glad to be an adult. By the time I left the ground it was five o'clock.

Chapter 9

By five or six o'clock on a Saturday it was usually safe to go home. They would all be so pissed they would hardly notice us, I was hoping Josh would return as well.

But the place was empty. Not a soul. I didn't give it too much thought at the time and went to my room. Two hours later, when Josh still hadn't returned, I crept down stairs and watched the telly, which was nice, it wasn't often I got the opportunity. They reckon that kids watch too much TV. Not in this house they don't. One television between four… and two of those four don't like kids being in the same room as them!

It was turning out to be weird day. Manic. Considering all my problems, things had turned out good… Old Bob, quality TV time and queer Deer shitting himself, almost getting it from Stick. But what about Stick? Why had he said that Josh had been arrested. He definitely hadn't, Bob was well in with the local law because of his job, and he'd have definitely found out if he had. And what about the two sisters?

Normally on a Saturday night I'd have met up with Mo and the rest, but I was having such a good time, watching anything I wanted, I didn't fancy it. I thought they might have at least texted though. As soon as Dad and Rosie returned, I'd go out.

At about eight thirty I heard what I thought was a knock at the door, but when I looked there was no one there, just a brown parcel. It wasn't addressed to anybody and I put it on the mantel piece, which was beside the telly… I could switch my eyes from the screen to the parcel and back to the screen without moving my head. That was a problem, because it looked as though there was money in it, and it was tempting me.

I examined it, it definitely felt like money, but it was sealed, and as much as I wanted to know how much was inside, anybody would have been able to tell if it'd been tampered with. This time I put it in the cupboard of the sideboard, so I'd forget about it, which I soon did.

I stayed up til I couldn't keep awake, then went to bed. Sunday morning came. I was starving. Slating myself for forgetting to eat anything at all the day before made me remember the other thing I'd forgotten about. I couldn't go out without letting Dad or Rosie know about it so, after I'd eaten some cornflakes, I grabbed the parcel and poked my head gingerly into their bedroom… it was empty. They hadn't come home, all night.

Suddenly I felt really alone.

Day 4 Sunday

I stashed the packet back in the cupboard and left the house. Sunday, I decided, was going to start like Saturday, riding the mono rail, only this time I'd combine it with thinking about my future and looking out for the sisters.

I felt much better, didn't feel as though someone had kicked hell out of my arse, and I didn't feel quite so down. I was thinking clearly, my state of mind was just right for solving problems. Right! Where was Josh? The last time I had seen him was Friday afternoon, when he said he'd be back in an hour. If he had seen Deer attacking me, Deer would have been in trouble, I'm sure of it, but he'd turned up in the park, as right as roses... til he was attacked by Stick. I decided to think that Josh didn't know a thing about it.

He hadn't been arrested. If he'd run away he'd have told me he was going to, so... he can only have been taken. That was the only option left. Kidnapped! That must have been why the police were at the house yesterday, because Dad had reported Josh missing. That would be why Dad and Rosie were away, they'd be looking for him. But this didn't make sense. There were a few things I couldn't get my head round: Old Bob would have been told this by the police; it would be well out of character for Dad to be concerned enough to be looking for him; why on earth would anybody want to kidnap Josh; and why had Stick lied?

The things I had to worry about were stacking up: I might be gay; the gang might find out I was gay; had Josh been kidnapped? I had to kill Michael Deer; I had to ask Stick why he had lied to me... Admittedly it wasn't a long list, but each worry on its own was enough for any man, and technically, I wasn't a man.

All this thinking had made me hungry. I'd travelled on the Central Line to Rowhedge and back to Severalls Park three times, with no sight of the sisters. I decided it was time to eat.

McDonald's, opposite the football ground, was my choice. I texted Mo to see if he fancied meeting me. He didn't get back. I tried Fallon. Then the others... nothing. I gulped down a large big mac before making my way across the park towards home, a little mystified as to why the others were not returning my texts.

Back home was still empty. I phoned Rosie's mobile and I heard it go off. It was in one of her coat pockets. That wasn't right! I couldn't try dad, I didn't know his number. Even if I did, I don't think I'd have phoned him.

I hung around for a while, but I was getting bored. What do people do if they're not in a gang? I tried the telly. I tried games on my mobile. I wished we had a computer. I even took my shirt off and lay on the back lawn. That was the most stupid thing I had done for a long time. All this and it was still only two o'clock. I could open the package… count the money.

In the top ten of stupid things to do, it was right up there with laying semi naked in the back garden. But I *had* laid. And I hadn't counted the money.

There was seven hundred and forty quid. No note, no nothing… just cash.

Chapter 10

There had been a food fare out along the High Street and at six o'clock all the stall holders were packing up. The place was a-buzz. The warm sunny weather had resulted in record crowds and record takings. I sat at one of the tables outside the High Street café to watch the proceedings but within minutes a waitress came across to move me on, I thought.

"Hello sir, would you like to order?"

What!

"Can I get you a coffee?"

"Err, I'll have a coke please."

"Diet?"

"No, a normal one," and she was off. This was highly unusual, we were always chased off. It was because I was on my own. The coke came and I paid. I was coming to the conclusion that it was quite nice not having the gang around for a change.

The air smelt good, of all the different foods of the market, and I began to feel peckish, even though I'd eaten the big mac earlier, and was leafing through the little menu. Though I didn't know what most of it was, written all posh, if I'd been forced to eat at the place I would have chosen one of three choices: Roasted red pepper hummus with feta cheese and mint oil, served with wedges; Slow roasted pork belly with a cider sauce; or Chicken boxty quesadilla, which was grilled chicken, tomato pico, pepper jack cheese, all between two potato boxties, drizzled with red chilli aioli and sour cream on the side.

"Food's good here."

A bloke has sat down at my table. I'd seen him, often. He was dressed all in red and had horns and a tail, even had red tights on. He was one of the street entertainers; a living statue. He placed his red mask on the table and the rest of his stuff beneath it.

"Do you mind me sitting here?"

Mind! It was brilliant. I couldn't believe he had chosen to sit at my table. I hoped and hoped that the gang would walk past, or Josh, especially Josh. The red devil was my favourite street artist.

"No."

"Are you eating, because I hate eating alone?"

"I don't know, hadn't decided." I wished he would put his mask on.

He fidgeted until he was comfortable. "What do you fancy?"

I showed him the three choices.

"I don't want that. Hummus. I like meat."

I thought it was meat, seeing how it was roasted.

"Now." There followed a long drawn out thought. "The other two though… I can't decide. What if we choose one of each and we dip into each other's?"

I just nodded.

"And I'll tell you what, we'll have a nice glass of chardonnay, how about that?"

I wasn't sure what chardonnay was so I agreed. He ordered.

While we waited for our food he lit up, offered me one and was genuinely pleased when I refused. "I'm Jeff," and we shook hands.

"Seen you before, loads of times, you're my favourite statue."

"Well thank you. Though I'm not really a statue, I move too much."

"It's brilliant though, what you do."

"Thanks. What about you, what do you do?"

"I'm at school."

"Okay is it, school?"

"Nah, not really. I'm thinking of leaving."

"To do what?"

I shrugged. "I thought maybe a job with the groundsman at the football ground."

"Colchester?"

"Yeah."

"Good team. Do you like gardening or something?"

"Not really, never done it. I know a little bit about grass though."

He laughed. "You should stay there, at school, for as long as you can. There's not a lot to life out in the big world these days, unless you're one of the lucky ones."

"I don't think it's doing me any good, staying on. And also I need to find somewhere to live, and you need money for that."

"I'd stay with your mum and dad for as long as you can… you *have* got a mum and dad?"

"I've got a dad. But I don't think I'll be staying with him for much longer."

"Really, why not?"

"Not very friendly."

The meals came, with wine. I wasn't sure if I was allowed and waited before I touched it. The food was alright, and Jeff was a good laugh, told me about his times as the horny red devil, how he went all over England and Europe doing his thing. I ate like Jeff and I drank like Jeff, and we had a second glass before we finished eating. We got on well, for some reason he liked me. After eating we relaxed. He had a coffee and I had another coke.

I don't know where I got the courage, but said, "Can you do the red devil for me, before you go?"

As soon as I said it I realised it wasn't the thing to ask, we'd eaten together like real friends, and now I'd spoiled everything.

"Yeah, of course I can, anything for you, little buddy," he laughed and put on his mask. He placed his box and his little dish in front of the café tables.

People had been looking at him the whole time we'd been sitting there, the man dressed as the horny red devil, and as soon as he put on his mask with the stupid grin there was a real stir, everybody seated at the tables was watching. He was a real showman and played to the crowd. He stood on the box, bowing and gesturing to them all, and to me, and pulling stupid, but nice, faces. Suddenly a lady stood up and aimed her camera at him. He froze.

His hand shot out and pointed towards her as though he was about to place some sort of spell. The camera clicked… and in the blink of the eye he collapsed into his box. It was incredible, one second he was there, the next, gone, and the box wasn't even big enough for him, but inside it he was. Everybody cheered and clapped. When he didn't come back out I remembered the trick. I pulled a pound coin from my pocket and placed it into his little dish. As soon as he heard the clink he was back out, up and standing on top of his box.

Suddenly there were loads of cameras. He stopped, pointed, and then disappeared again. There was a stampede of people rushing to the dish and soon it was overflowing, notes as well. Jeff climbed out of his box, bowed to the crowd, whipped off his mask and returned to the table.

He slipped the dish-full of money under the mask and winked. "That will pay for our supper."

I was so happy I could have cried. He did that for me! Twenty minutes later, he was gone, and my world was back as it was before I sat down.

.

Chapter 11

I had another coke. One of the things that struck me was, as people got up and left, they all said something, goodbye, all the best mate, and such things. This was all new to me, this pleasantness. Normally people swore and told me to bugger off.

The traders had gone by now and a big clean-up operation was in progress, but the cafés and bars still had plenty of people milling around outside, drinks in hand and laughing and chatting away... I was ambling down the High Street contemplating this, and my time with Jeff. Up to now, fun had generally been at other peoples' expense, taking the piss, shoving things through letter boxes, winding people up. The only people who found it funny was us, the castle gang.

Is this normal life, all this friendliness? Have I missed all this because I've been running around in a gang? Maybe I've been wasting my life... things must change. What the fuck! I was almost bowled over.

"You've got to help."

I couldn't believe it, it was the small sister! She wrapped her arms around me, her head in my chest. "Please. Please," she begged.

Words failed me. I'd spent almost two days hoping for a chance meeting and resigning myself to the horrible conclusion that I'd never see them again… And now. This.

"Please, help."

I pushed her back, gently.

"I remember you from the mono rail. You look really nice."

She tried to smile. She looked distressed.

"Okay…"

"Follow me… please, we need your help."

I hoped that *we* meant her and her sister. She tugged at my arm.

I followed her as she scuttled down a small ally, Bank Passage. It led to the back of the High Street shops, where it was more officy than shops, it was deserted. Behind some bins was her sister, sitting on a low wall. She'd obviously been crying. The small one bounded over to her… "It's alright now. I've found someone to help us."

Again I was speechless. Helping blonds in trouble was out of my comfort zone. This was weird, what was wrong? They both looked at me, expecting me to say something.

"Hello."

They both stared, obviously wanting more.

I cleared my throat… "Are you alright?" Fucking stupid. "What's the problem?"

The sister looked angry. "Emma, what's the matter with you, this dick-head can't help us, he's a little boy."

That was a bit rich, if she was older than me, it wasn't by much.

Emma protested. "He will." She looked at me, "won't you?"

"I don't know, what do you want?"

"You got any money?"

I didn't answer straight away.

"See, he's wasting our time. I told you to find somebody who could help."

"I've got some money."

The sister glared. "How much?"

I pulled out the notes, "Thirty-five quid, plus some coins."

"Oh God… that's no good."

"It'll help," said Emma, "maybe he's got friends."

They both looked at me in silence, waiting for a response. Yeah, I had friends, but what would they say, if it wasn't fuck off. They'd want to know more. A lot more.

"Why do you want money?"

They both looked at each other.

"If you want to borrow money, I need to know why. I need to know how much, an' I need to know if I'll get it back."

The sister mellowed. "I'm sorry. It's okay. This is our problem. It's not fair to involve you."

I looked at the both of them. They *were* beautiful. If we were going to be an item, their problems were my problems.

"It's our things," said Emma, "the bloke who rented us a room wants four hundred pounds before he'll let us have them."

"The problem is," continued the sister, "I can get money from our uncle but my phonebook and mobile is with the stuff, and unless I've got them, there's nothing I can do. I can't remember the phone number."

"Why does he want four hundred quid?"

"Our rent… that's what we owe him."

"Can't you talk to him? Explain that you need your phone to get the money."

"He won't listen."

"Can't you get the number from anywhere else?"

"No."

"118 118."

"Ex-directory."

"Is your stuff worth four hundred quid?" That was a good question and I was chuffed I asked it.

"Of course it is… it's all we have, everything."

Sorry. "An' will I get the money back? If I can get it."

The small one rushed over and put her arms around me again. "I knew you'd help. I knew it Dais."

"Dais?"

"Daisy," said the older sister, "my name."

"Oh. Anyway, I don't know if I can get it."

"But you might, you can try," said Dais.

Fuck. What had I let myself in for? I knew I could get the money… providing Dad and Rosie were still away. "How long would you need it for?"

"Can you get it then?"

"I might be able to. But how long will you need it for?"

"When can you get it?"

"If I can get it, then soon."

"Tonight?"

I nodded.

"Okay then. Tomorrow, this time. We'll give you all of it back by nine o'clock tomorrow night. Here," she pulled off her necklace. "You can keep this, until you get your money back."

"Is it worth anything?"

"Yes. But more than that, it's sentimental. It's a St Christopher. My dad gave it to me, the last time I saw him… it's my good luck charm. So, to me, it's worth a fortune."

I told her to put it back on… it didn't look as though it was worth much. I had to trust them.

I could go and then not come back, forget them. But they looked so needy, and I felt good being able to help.

If I could. Still, I figured I had nothing to lose.

The house was still empty. I had already decided that even if they were back they wouldn't have known about the cash and I could have sneaked out with it. However, they weren't back.

I took the lot.

Chapter 12

I don't know what I expected after I'd handed over five hundred quid; four for the rent and one so they'd be able to eat and get a room for the night... they couldn't sleep on the street! I just felt there should have been more than a whoop and a peck on the cheek, but that's all there was... peck peck... gone. I thought I might have eaten with them, at least, but I supposed they were in a rush to get their things.

As I walked towards home I began to fret. If Dad and Rosie returned to find the cash missing I'd be in big trouble, however much I protested that I knew nothing about it. The problem was... taking the money was the first time I'd ever stolen anything in my life. When I replaced it, I'd have only borrowed it, but until that time...

When I replaced it! When? That was the moment it dawned on me. I'd been taken for a ride. I almost collapsed. Suddenly everything that had previously been worrying me vanished, to be replaced by the realisation that I was a complete moron. A person who had just given five hundred quid to two complete strangers. A person who was going to die, or at least be severely beaten and thrown out onto the streets.

The park was closed so I ran up and down the adjacent streets about a thousand times. I couldn't stop. How this was ever going to help my situation, I had no idea, but it was the best I could come up with at the time.

If anybody had been watching they would have thought that I'd gone mad. Caught some terrible disease and… What if I had aids? God, was there no end to the misery I seemed able to pile on myself? I almost collapsed through sheer exhaustion… just made it to a small wall and sat down. And when I was sat I started to do the thing I should have done long before; think! And at that moment that was the last thing I wanted to do.

What the hell was I going to do now?

It wasn't long before I began to feel cold and wondered what the days ahead held for me. I really didn't fancy the idea of sleeping rough and that made me feel a little better about giving the money to the sisters, maybe they're not con artists, maybe I really had saved them from a cold night. Tomorrow would tell.

What I was thinking, I don't know, but I hid the rest of the money in a hole in the wall and I dragged myself home. The cloudless skies meant the temperature dropped quickly as darkness set in and I really hoped that Dad hadn't returned from wherever he'd been. I couldn't face him. All I wanted was to slide into bed and forget about my disease, my being a moron, being gay, the kidnapping of Josh, the death of Michael Deer, homelessness… and Dad and Rosie. Where were they?

All those worries, bad as they were, disappeared as I turned on the lights in the living room. Squeezed into Dad's chair in the corner of the room was the hardest looking guy I'd ever seen… shaved, polished head, thick black unbuttoned Crombie, size twenty DM's and knuckles as big as my head.

I stepped back, as much in surprise as anything else, only to be shoved back into the centre of the room by his twin.

"Where's yer old man?"

"I, I don't know."

With that answer I was given a gentle smack around the back of my head, which sent me flying across the room. The one who administered the tap picked me up by my clothing with one hand, and with my feet off the ground the seated one asked again.

"Where's yer old man?"

I needed a different answer. "Put me down. Please."

Amazingly the guy lowered me to the floor and stood back.

"I don't know," and before he could hit me again I dropped to the floor, hoping that saving him the trouble of knocking me down would please him.

Without showing any displeasure or otherwise, he picked me up, dusted me down, stepped back… and then hit me.

Sometime later, I don't know how long, I came round and found myself snugly sitting on the sofa… between the both of them.

"Look. Just tell us where yer old man is an' we won't hurt yer."

I forced myself to start crying, for sympathy. I think this annoyed them more… watching a grown kid blubbering away obviously disgusted them. The thought of getting snot all over their fists kept them from hitting me around the head, instead they each took a leg, just above the knee, and squeezed. My screams didn't bring anybody rushing to the door. Finally they came to the conclusion that I really didn't know where my Dad was.

"Tell yer old man that if Charlie Farthin don't get his money, he'll be dead."

"Who'll be dead?"

"Yer fuckin dad," and he again slapped me playfully round the head.

They left me snivelling on the chair. In all, they'd only been in my company for a few minutes, but in those few minutes they had made a real impression…

I locked and bolted the doors, I didn't care that Dad and Rosie wouldn't be able to get in, and went to bed for another sleepless night.

That was a weekend I'll never forget. At about five in the morning I went and got the two hundred and forty quid that I'd hidden the night before. It had been a good move not to take it back to the house because I'm sure the fuckers, Farthin's fuckers, searched me while I was knocked out. Why was I in this trouble? Was it all connected? Was any of it connected?

Who is Charlie Farthin?

Day 5 Monday

Another warm and sunny day. I didn't go to school. I didn't even go to the park. I stayed at home, in my room. A couple of times there were knocks at the door but there was no way I was going to talk to anybody. I think I did sleep some, dropped off every now and then. But the weight of my worries didn't let me rest for long.

How were they connected? Being gay, being diseased, Michael Deer. They were connected. The cash coming through the front door, Dad going missing, Charlie Farthin, even Josh disappearing. They were completely separate from the first pile, but… could they be connected with each other? The sisters… and me ending up on the streets for being a moron were obviously connected, but they were entirely of my own making. The dark bruising on my thighs matched my sombre mood. Again, I thought about ending it all… living was becoming too difficult, and the thought of having no worries was attractive. I kept weighing one against the other.

By mid-afternoon I was so hungry I'd forgotten about topping myself. There was nothing in the fridge, not even milk or bread. At the same time I felt too weak to go out and get anything, especially with the bother of having to do it while I didn't know how many arseholes would be trying to send me back to school.

We'd learnt about the first world war in history and I thought of the women who used to hand out white feathers to men walking the streets. It didn't matter that those men might have been home on leave, even recovering from injuries received at the front, or older lads still at school, mutilation and death months, or even years, away. In the eyes of those women, they were all cowards. The women didn't bother to try and find out about a guy's background, or his problems. They just thrust a feather into his face, so much so that even soldiers who had shot themselves to get away from that bloodbath and death, preferred to go back.

Well… let them try and thrust a feather in my face. Fuck them! Sisters in arms.

But no-one bothered me. I didn't have too much of a choice, the chippie and the other take-aways were all closed, being half way through the afternoon on a Monday, so it was McDonald's again.

Chapter 13

While eating I thought about going to the police, about Josh. The law had never been our friends during my lifetime. Never any friendly banter with the gang, no. It was always a case of moving us on, booking one of us for something or other, asking about a recent piece of vandalism or a break-in somewhere. The law in our world is what we dish out ourselves. Or that's what we're always told, although I never quite knew what that meant, other than you never went to the police... for anything.

But, I couldn't just sit back wondering where Josh was, whether he had been kidnapped. He could be chained up in some weirdo's cellar waiting to be saved, except, nobody knew he had been taken, apart from his stupid brother. Even that line of thinking didn't work though, and I didn't go and report it.

Dad and Rosie were next on the thinking list. I couldn't imagine Dad wasting his time looking for a missing son, but the thought kept nagging at me, that their disappearance and Josh's were connected. But how?

Out of nowhere, Fallon appeared.

"Saw you from outside. You gonna buy me a Mac?"

"Hiya." I didn't even ask her why she wasn't at school, I was that pleased to see one of the gang. I brought another meal for myself and one for her.

"Where you been?" I asked, "I've been texting everyone all weekend."

"We've been about. Trouble is the others got pissed down by the river on Saturday night, so pissed that they were all ill yesterday."

"They go to school today?"

She shrugged. "I had to go and see some cousins on Saturday, or I'd have been with em. What about you?"

"I stayed in an' watched telly."

"What?"

"I stayed in. Rosie an' Dad have gone somewhere an' I had the place to myself, so I stayed in."

"I wish my fuckin mum an' dad would fuck off an' me not to have to go with em. I could have come and stayed with you."

"And watched telly."

"If you say so," and she slid a long chip backwards and forwards through her lips... seductively, I think. Another day I'd have been all over her, in my mind. But not this time. What did that say?

"Fallon. They've gone, disappeared, left… without a word, an' they've been gone all weekend."

"Really?"

"And Josh is gone."

"Gone, what, with em?"

"No, I don't think so. Josh was gone when I got up on Saturday morning. Dad an' Rosie were still at home then."

"But now they've gone?"

"Yeah."

"An' they didn't say where?"

"No."

"Or when they'd be back?"

"No."

"Fuck." She shoved a pile of chips into her mouth and chewed for a while. "What about the police?"

"Stick told me that Josh had been arrested."

"Well then, that's where he is."

"No he's not, I checked."

"What did he say it for then?"

"Don't know."

"Weird fucker, is Stick."

"You said it."

"Did you know his dad beats him up."

"No way."

"Fuckin true. That's why he's such a weird fucker, always got something to prove, to himself probably." She tipped the dregs of her coke and the ice into her mouth.

"Do you know who Charlie Farthin is?"

"Why?"

"Do you know?"

"Don't you?"

"No. I wouldn't be asking if I did."

"Well, you should know. He's a really nasty bastard, sells second hand cars, but only as a front. If it's dodgy, he's into it." She helped herself to one of my chips. "He's got a nice looking wife who had a fling with this bloke an' when Farthin found out he gave the bloke an ultimatum... hand over five grand or be killed."

"Fuck... what happened?"

"I dunno. He handed over the five grand I suppose."

"An' what about his wife?"

"She's alright. I reckon Farthin put her up to it."

"My old man owes him money."

Fallon didn't say anything.

"Two geezers were at my house last night, looking for him."

"Oh shit."

"Knocked me about a bit, wanting to know where they'd gone."

"Fuck. You okay?"

"You should see my legs."

"What, where they kicked you?"

"No, they fuckin tortured me by squeezing my thighs, the bastards."

"You should have made something up."

"I didn't think of that. I thought they were going to kill me."

"You've had a crap weekend."

"Not all crap." And I told her about the horny red devil and how he treated me to a meal.

I could see she was impressed. "I'd like to see the bruises, but I ain't coming back to your place, not with Charlie Farthin hanging around."

"Don't worry, I ain't got time to show you, got other things to see to."

"Like what?"

Me and my mouth, but fortunately I was thinking quick. "I'm gonna call on Josh's mates, an' anyone else who might know something."

"It wouldn't take long to show me your bruises."

I wasn't in the mood to flash my legs, but I had to act normal, for future sake. If the word got out I was gay at least Fallon would find it hard to believe. We went across to the Sports Centre and slipped into one of the toilets and I showed her my bruises for about twenty minutes, until some bloke said he was going to call security unless we packed up what we were doing and pissed off.

I was in two minds about going home but I wanted to collect the two hundred and forty quid left over from the package. I wasn't sure what I was going to do with it, but I wanted it with me.

Fallon had taken my mind off my worries, and had also reassured me a little about my sexuality. But as I pushed open the front door those worries flooded back with the fear that some bastard could be waiting inside. There was no-one. I grabbed a padded jacket, remembering how cold it got the night before, and the cash. I was about to leave when I noticed another package on the door mat… Did I miss it or had somebody pushed it through the letter box, knowing I was in? Was it some sort of trap?

There was nobody outside, anywhere. I made a decision and grabbed it from the floor and slipped away. School was over and there was no need to worry about roaming squads of women, just Charlie Farthin, his thugs and Michael Deer. And I didn't really want to bump into any of the castle gang either. I needed to be alone to meet the sisters. I had to hope I was wrong about them.

I jumped onto the Central Line and sat at the back of the last car, so that nobody could surprise me, and made my way to Rowhedge. The pits, that's where I was going to hide out for an hour or so. I found a brilliant place next to a large pool, completely hidden. Suddenly I felt good, like I was alone in the wilds. I was safe here. I opened the package. A thousand quid! This time though, there was a note.

I know it's not all there yet. Don't come looking for Josh or you won't get the rest.

What did this mean? It wasn't a demand from a kidnapper… it was more like somebody was paying for him. They had sold him! Dad had fucking sold Josh!

So. Dad owed Charlie Farthin money and had sold Josh so that he could pay him back. Now Dad and Rosie had disappeared and Farthin was annoyed. Why had they gone if they knew money was coming? Whatever their plan was, it had gone wrong. And who the fuck would buy Josh? And what for?

I wrapped the one thousand, two hundred and forty quid in the thick brown envelope paper, hid it safely under a pile of stones and made a mental note where it was.

Then I went back into Colchester.

Chapter 14

I got to Bank Passage an hour before I needed to, and waited. Three hours passed with no sign of the sisters. Unlike the night before there seemed to be plenty of people walking by, using the Passage as a short cut after working late I suppose, and I couldn't help myself, more than a few times my heart jumped in anticipation. But no. They didn't appear.

I didn't hurry and got back to the house at midnight, thinking that things couldn't get any worse! Well. Things can always get worse.

Charlie Farthin's sitting thug was in the living room again, same chair, same clothes, same shiny head. I didn't step back this time. I didn't want a smack around the head again. I just stood in resignation.

"Where's yer old man?"

I didn't answer. I wasn't being brave, I'd just had enough of being scared. It seemed that he was alone. In theory that evened things up a bit, put us on a level footing. Ha.

"I've been doin' some askin' around an' it seems that yer dad ain't been around for a few days."

I fucking told him that.

"And I've also learned that you an' im don't get on much."

Where was this going?

"Are you okay for cash?"

"You gonna lend me some money?"

"No. Mista Farthin is worried about ya, that's all." He stuck out a hand with some tenners in it. "Take it. It's not a loan, it's a gift. A hundred nicka. Take it, an' my mobile number, an' when yer dad comes back, or yer hear from him, let me know."

I took the cash, but only because it would be a waste of time refusing, and stood there like a lemon, staring at the notes in my hand.

"Look boy, I'm sorry about last night. Take the cash, an' consider Mista Farthin as yer fairy god-father. Do what he says an' you'll have some handy friends. Call me as soon as yer know anything an' ya won't be sorry." He stood. I thought he was going to sling his arms around me, but he went to the kitchen and turned on the kettle. He beckoned me to follow.

We sat in the small room and he told me that Dad had borrowed four thousand quid. How it worked was the loan would cost five hundred, so dad had to repay four and half thousand, and it had been due by the weekend. Every day after that the amount went up by five hundred, to pay for the extras incurred, like thugs having to be used to get it back, so now he owed five and a half thousand.

"My brother's disappeared as well."

"Older?"

"Eleven."

"How old are you?"

"Fifteen," there was a moment of silence, "sixteen in December."

He switched back to Josh. "He's probably gone with em."

"No. I don't think so." There was no way I was going to tell him that packets of cash had been dropping through the letter box, but I had to mention Josh in case Farthin and his gang knew anything.

I think he detected my concerns. "Look. Yer got me number. Call me for anything, Mista Farthin won't mind. Any problems yer have are now our problems."

Fuck!

And that was it really. After the cuppa and some more strained conversation he left me feeling weird about things. He said I'd meet Mr Farthin soon and that I'd like him. If I trusted him, I would have a good friend for life, and that Charlie Farthin was a very good friend to have, and a very bad enemy.

As I lay in bed, the thought of Charlie Farthin's thugs paying Michael Deer a visit kept going through my mind... I'd have to be there, to introduce them to him. But that meant I would have to tell my new friends I was gay, or if I wasn't gay, that I'd been with a gay bloke. I just decided that I had to be thankful that things had turned out the way they had.

Day 6 Tuesday

The next day I went to school. I wasn't expecting anything different, I didn't think about it, just turned up. But nobody spoke to me. All the kids seemed to turn away as I passed them, some sniggering as they did so. Even Mo and the gang were icy. Mo didn't sit beside me either.

At the first opportunity I tried to approach him. "What's up Mo?"

"Don't fuckin speak to me dick head."

I couldn't believe what I was hearing. In confusion, I stepped closer to him. A mistake. The next thing I knew I was on the ground, his hand had whacked me and I hadn't seen it coming. They were all there, standing around me, Stick, Fallon, Lee, Spider, Franny… and Mo. They weren't laughing though, just standing, and looking sad. After a while they all turned and walked away, leaving me sitting on the floor and thousands of other kids looking on. Everything was silent.

I legged it. Ran through the gates… Crazy Cameron, the school security wanker, shouting after me.

My head was spinning. I had no idea what had happened. There had been no piss-take. The couple of sniggers from other kids might have been a clue, but I couldn't figure it.

Was it because I was gay… spent the weekend apart from them… because I met the horny red devil… or because I was now part of Charlie Farthin's gang? Whatever the reason, it was unjustified. I was broken hearted.

I spent the day at Rowhedge. I had twenty-four quid of my own money, plus the extra hundred and, with the other cash, I was okay for finances. I decided to break out on my own, leave Dad, Rosie, the castle gang and school behind me. I'd think about 'Mista Farthin' later… he might come in handy! I also decided to give the sisters one more try, and in the evening I made my way back into Colchester.

As it was still light I slipped back and got some stuff from the house… brush and toothpaste, matches, garlic, anything I thought might come in handy and could carry easily. Then I walked to Bank Passage and waited.

I was there by eight. It was another long three hours while I waited for the bitches to show. Funny thing was though, I wasn't that upset. I knew they wouldn't turn up, and now that I'd made my mind up that I was never going home again, being conned out of five hundred quid didn't seem to matter that much anymore.

I left it as long as I could before catching the mono, before they shut down, and got back to the pits around midnight.

I'd found some plastic and made a roof for my new home. I hung the garlic at the 'doorway', stashed the duvet cover I'd brought with me into a couple of big plastic bags and climbed in amongst it, and before I could dream about football I'd fallen asleep.

Day 7 Wednesday

It was light when I woke up, after the best night's sleep I could remember. I should have become homeless long before this. I was warm and comfortable as the sun streaked into my hideout. I even saw a fox. I was sure that, sooner or later, I'd be reported as missing, so I had to be alert, but for the moment I considered myself free. It didn't really matter about anything, other than Josh. I didn't care about being gay; it was just the way I was. Even Michael Deer was no longer an issue, knowing I could have him blown away with just a phone call.

And Stick, and Mo, and Fallon, and the rest of the castle gang? I'd grown apart from them. The weekend had definitely been better without them. The crap would still have happened, even the sisters, but I'd learnt from everything. School wasn't for me anymore. Now that I'd left the gang I'd be invisible anyway. My only purpose for living now was to find Josh.

I wrapped the cash in a plastic bag and re-hid it before getting cleaned up (I must get some bottles of water) and caught the mono back into Colchester. I got myself a notebook and pen and had some breakfast in a café and began to jot down everything that might mean something regarding finding Josh, including my rape (in case it mattered), the cash (times of drops), when dad and Rosie disappeared, Charlie Farthin's thugs. Anything that could be a factor. Fuck. What a waste of time, it was like being at school. What was the matter with me? I threw away the notebook, vowing never to write anything. Ever. Again.

I had the money for a laptop, I could get a page on Facebook. Then I thought about life without electricity. My mobile needed charging.

Although I said I'd never return to the house, this was important. I slipped back and put the phone on charge and then wandered over to the park, ending up at the clump of bushes where I'd last seen Josh, and Stick had nearly done Deer.

Life was pretty good, laying in the sun. I missed the gang though. Why had· Mo hit me? My mind was empty, no dreams, no plans, no memories. It was like I time travelled forward three hours, one minute it was ten o'clock, the next it was the usual spew-out of students and workers onto the grassy slopes for lunch break. I should be watching everything.

I decided that I ought to go to the police. The trouble was… if I went during school hours, they'd send me back. I decided to go that evening. When I collected the mobile and charger there was another package on the doormat; seven hundred and sixty this time. And there was another note.

This makes it 2500. Don't ever contact us.

So Josh had been sold. That's it. Kaput. Done… I left the house, this time doubly vowing never to go back, never to see Dad or Rosie again. Never.

Chapter 15

I got ten yards from the gate when I decided to go back and grab a couple of things, a picture of Josh and a pillow, and after buying some crisps and biscuits and sweets and drinks, I made my way back to Rowhedge. I should've kept the notebook and made a list, then I wouldn't have forgotten the water.

So I made a mental note to buy some water and some comics next time I went to Colchester, to the cop shop. I didn't want to go into town too early in case I bumped into Mo or anybody and I was getting bored just watching dog walkers. One dog came into my place and wouldn't leave, the fucker. He tried to piss on Josh's photo. I had to make out I was just walking alongside the pool, to take it back to its owner. Dogs might be a problem in the future, perhaps I shouldn't hang around during the day.

I hopped on the mono and went across the river to Wivenhoe, a fishing village like Rowhedge but with more people wandering about. It had a shop with comics. The one I chose was Mai, the Psychic Girl, who's a 14-year-old Japanese girl with powerful psychic abilities. She's being chased by the Wisdom Alliance, an organization that strives to control the world. The Alliance already controls four other powerful psychic children, and it has hired the Kaieda Intelligence Agency to capture Mai.

It was awesome, but I didn't get to read much of it. There were some benches by the jetty and I made myself comfortable on one, with the intention of finding out more about Mai. In order to find the Psychic Girl, the KIA followed her sister, hoping that she would eventually lead him to their target.

Who would lead *me* to Josh? And suddenly reading comics became unimportant. Who? I couldn't relax. All I knew was, he disappeared after Michael Deer attacked me. Would I get anywhere by tailing Deer?

I had nothing to lose… why not give it a go? it would be better than going to the cops! Tomorrow I'd go to Castle Park and watch out for the fat bastard and follow him. And I decided to go to Bank Passage again, give the sisters one last chance.

I arrived at dead on nine, not very hopeful, and resigned to another wasted evening. I plonked myself onto the wall where Dais had sat when I saw her on Sunday. There was something at my feet, written on the pavement in black marker ink. D AND E… Dais and Emma? If it meant anything, I didn't know what. I was squatted at the message (if it was one), trying to figure it out, when guess who crept up behind me and covered my eyes with their hands. "Guess who?"

It was the fucking sisters! The fucking fucking fucking sisters! And they were happy to see me as well. They weren't con artists, they were just sisters. I'd known it all along.

Dais had got hold of her mobile and had managed to contact her uncle, but there'd been complications, they wouldn't say what, but they hadn't got back to Colchester until this morning and they'd come to Bank Passage this evening, hoping I'd be here.

I knew they weren't con artists.

They gave me the five hundred quid.

I knew all along they weren't con artists.

And they gave me twenty extra; interest, which I tried not to take, but they insisted.

They were never, ever, con artists.

I walked with a sister on each arm, and they in turn were loaded down with satchels on their shoulders and pulling big suit cases on wheels. Three homeless kids! They wanted to eat so I suggested the café where I'd spent time with the red devil. It was after nine and getting parky, so we sat inside and we all ordered the roasted pork belly with a cider sauce. With my fingers crossed under the table I asked for a bottle of chardonnay, and got it.

Over a glass each, I made them both laugh when I told them about the red devil.

"When is he coming back?" asked Emma.

"Don't know. He definitely is though, sometime. He said he was performing across Europe for a few weeks."

Dais was more interested in where I lived. "Where is your house?"

"Not far, just the other side of the park."

"Oh." It was said enviously, thinking I had a place to stay.

"I'm not living there though. I'm staying in Rowhedge."

"You have two places!"

"I've left home. My dad's a shit, he doesn't like me an' also he's sold my brother."

"Sold, what do you mean?"

"Just what I said, he's sold Josh. He owes money to a bloke called Charlie Farthin, an' to raise the money to repay him, he's sold Josh. But he obviously didn't get enough an' Farthin's hard cases keep calling at the house looking for him. So I'm not going back."

"So they haven't got your dad yet."

"No, him an' my step mum have scarpered, I haven't seen em since Saturday."

"God."

"So, where's this place in Rowhedge?"

"It isn't a place, it's a… well, it is a place, but not a house. It's a bit of ground by a pond, I've made it a home, got pictures an' everything. If you had sleeping bags you could stay with me."

"Yuck," said Emma, "spiders and creepy crawlies. I'm not staying there."

"What do Charlie Farthin's guys do, you know, when they see you?" asked Dais.

"The first time they tortured me, tried to make me tell em where dad was."

"And you didn't tell them."

"I didn't know. After though, the next day, one of em came back an' said he knew I was telling the truth an' Charlie Farthin was sorry I was hurt an' gave me a hundred quid an' said I was to keep in touch with him."

"So you could go back to the house."

"No, my dad might come back."

"It doesn't sound as though he will, does it?"

I didn't know. But if he did!

"I don't think he'll come back. We could all stay there."

"But if he does he'll kill me."

"Why, because of me and Emma."

"No, cos I've got the two an' a half grand that was paid for Josh. Someone's been posting it through our front door, three packs with it in. That's how I was able to lend you five hundred."

"You've stolen it?"

"To start with I borrowed it. But when I found out where it came from, I decided to keep it, to try an' buy Josh back."

"Do you know who's got him then?"

"No."

"Does your dad, or this Charlie Farthin, know you've got the money?"

"No."

"So we could stay, and if your dad comes back you can tell him that Charlie Farthin's blokes have been around and that they tortured you and that you don't know anything about any money and he'll assume that Charlie Farthin has got it."

That sounded pretty sound to me. "What about you two?"

"Tell him we're paying rent."

"He'll want the money."

"Then we'll have to tell him we're not paying much."

The food came.

"We *could* actually pay you rent, if we stay."

"Why would you want to do that?"

"Well… we should."

"Well… you don't have to."

"So we can stay then?"

"I thought you were."

Later we talked about Josh, what he was like. "How are you going to find him?"

This was dodgy ground. I planned to follow Michael Deer, but if I told them that, they'd want to know what the connection was… why? "I don't know yet."

"Have you been to the police?"

"I don't trust em." They seemed to accept this and I wondered why.

"What about you two? Why are you in Colchester?"

"Because of Richard," answered Emma.

"Richard's an arsehole," said Dais. "He's our mum's bloke and he isn't very nice."

"Not nice?"

"No. Not nice."

"In what way?"

"It doesn't matter, he's just not nice. I decided to come to Colchester because there's supposed to be work here, and there was no way Emma was going to stay behind without me."

"Couldn't you go to your uncle, the one who lent you money?"

"He's sweet, but scared. If Richard found out about him helping us there'd be real trouble. For that reason, he doesn't even want to know where we are, as long as we're alright."

It sounded as though we all had our problems. I realised then that we'd be better off sticking together. Up to that point I felt that I'd been manoeuvred into letting them stay with me in the house… but now I knew it was best thing for all of us.

Chapter 16

It was almost midnight when we arrived at the house. In darkness and obviously empty, I still felt sick in the stomach as I crept towards its front door. When I said 'obviously empty', I meant 'of people' but I had the shock of my life when I went through the door. It was empty! Not one stick of furniture. No chairs, no beds, table, television, kettle, toaster, oven, washing machine… not even any clothes, curtains, sheets… and no toilet paper. The whole house had been stripped of everything.

"I didn't expect this," said Dais, as me and Emma gawped open mouthed.

"I was here this afternoon, everything was here then." I walked back out onto the street and looked up and down it. All I saw was Mrs Smith, our curtain twitching neighbour twitching her curtain.

"We can still stay, the carpets are still here and the heating and electric still works."

"I wonder who's taken it all."

"Your dad?"

"Could have been. Maybe he came back after dark."
But, to be honest, I had no idea. Perhaps Charlie
Farthin had taken it, in lieu of what he was owed. "I
think we should stay upstairs in the big bedroom, the
window faces the back an' the light's not so likely to be
seen from outside."

"Okay," said Dais, "rule number one, no lights on,
except in the bedroom… and then only when the door
is shut."

We all traipsed up the stairs, pulling the girls
belongings behind, and into the bedroom, closed the
door and flicked on the light. We piled all the stuff in
the centre of the floor and sat cross legged around it.
Emma pulled out a thick woollen top, slumped
sideways and, using it as a pillow, was soon asleep.

Me and Dais talked and talked. She told me about
how her mum wanted her and Emma *out the way* when
Richard appeared on the scene. It was a loveless family,
she said. I told her about my life, or most of it, and we
both agreed that we had a lot in common, shared a
loveless existence. I wished we, me, her and Emma,
could be a family. "I think we shall be," she said. She
held me close to her, and that's how we slept.

Day 8 Thursday

When I awoke, it was light… and I was alone. All the
stuff was still piled on the floor though. I laid on my

back as I slowly came round and realised that I'd slept well, and all night! Perhaps I wasn't made to sleep on beds. I could hear movement around the house, the sisters. The bedroom door opened and bright sunlight streaked into the room from the front of the house, followed by Dais, wearing a floppy shirt and not much else, as far as I could tell, anyway.

"Morning."

I smiled a reply. My eyes followed her around the room as she opened different bags and cases looking for something or other, she didn't care that I watched her every move. She was beautiful, all over. Then Emma came in. "Have you found it yet?"

"No, you sure you didn't leave it in the hotel?"

"No." She shoved her hand into a satchel and pulled out a small bag. "Here, toothbrushes as well," and they both walked from the room.

I heard them giggling. I wondered what they were up to.

They had both left the room, but their images hadn't. I closed my eyes and watched them wandering around me as I drifted back to sleep. I felt warm and safe. But it didn't last long.

In they came, first Dais then Emma. "Come on you," said Emma, "time to get up," and she stepped over me and took my hands and tried to pull me from the floor.

"Lazy bones," said Dais, and they each took one of my hands and pulled me to my feet.

They were so close, and so natural. Emma kissed me good morning and they got themselves ready for the day ahead.

"I've run a bath for you," said Dais. "While you're washing, we're going to the shop to get some breakfast and a few bits and pieces, like mugs and things, anything you need?"

What a question.

As I lay in the sudsy water, I thought about all the things that had happened since my last bath and realised why Dais had suggested I had one now, it had been nearly a week. I washed my socks and pants in my water and hung them over the sink while I soaked at leisure. Life was weird. That thought crossed my mind, along with what I should be planning, but most of my brain space was filled with beautiful, sexy sisters.

I hadn't been soaking for long, I'd topped up a couple of times with hot water, when I heard the front door slam. I thought it was them, until I heard the voice.

"What the fuck…"

It was Dad. I jumped from the bath and pulled my jeans on over what would have been an embarrassment had he barged into the bathroom. The sisters were forgotten, but it takes a bit longer for other parts of the body to realise that.

Sheepishly I emerged from the small room.

"What the fuck's going on?" from the bottom of the stairs.

106

"What?"

"The fuckin furniture… where is it?"

"I thought you took it."

"You fuckin idiot, why would I take it?"

He bounded up the stairs, pushed me aside and checked the bedrooms. "What's all this?" pointing to the pile of stuff on the floor.

"It's mine."

"No it fuckin isn't," and he emptied a case, girl's clothes spilling onto the carpet.

"Charlie Farthin." I said. He froze.

"What about Charlie Farthin?"

"His blokes call every morning, looking for you."

Dad stood… obviously giving this little lie some consideration.

"I think it was them that took everything."

He was stunned into silence, all I was telling him made sense.

"Christ." He kicked at the clothing, not a violent kick, just a little sort of toe-poke. "An' these?"

"His nieces. He said they had to stay here and contact him as soon as you showed up."

He lost a little colour. "Did he talk to you?"

"His blokes did. They tortured me, trying to find out where you an' Rosie had gone. But I didn't tell em, cos I didn't know."

He just looked at me. I think he felt guilty about running off and leaving without saying anything.

"Where's Josh?" I asked.

Suddenly he was back to his old self. "He's fuckin gone. Forget about him, forget he ever existed."

"He's my brother." I stepped forward, "how can I just forget him?"

I saw it coming, tried to duck, but he caught me on the side of the face and as I fell his knee smashed into my head. He bent over, squeezed a hand around my neck and picked me up. "Don't fuckin tell Farthin you've seen me you little shit," and threw me back to the floor. "An' you can tell them fuckin nieces that if they say anything to Farthin I'll kill em."

If you're so fuckin hard, why don't *you* go and face Farthin, I wanted to say, but didn't.

He checked in the other bedrooms. Then the ground floor, swearing all the time. The front door was nearly slammed off its hinges as he left the house. My face was covered in blood and snot and tears, so I slipped back into the bath and cleaned myself up. I wished he was dead.

I didn't hear the front door open as the sisters returned, which was probably a good thing, I might have had a heart attack. I heard them chatting and clattering about and I decided to haul myself from the water, but before I could, Emma barged into the bathroom a plonked herself on the pan.

"I can't believe you're still in the bath."

I smiled.

"What's the matter, are you alright?" She studied my face. "Dais."

Dais poked her head around the door.

"Look Dais." Dais looked.

"God, what happened?"

"My dad came home." The news startled them.

"It's okay though, he's gone, an' I don't think he'll be back."

"Did he do that?" meaning my face.

I nodded.

"What did he want?"

Actually I didn't know. "Whatever it was he didn't get it, he just had a look round, beat me up a bit, an' left."

"What about our stuff?"

"It's all right, he started to look in your cases, but stopped when I told him you were Charlie Farthin's nieces an' that you were here so that you could let Farthin know when he returned."

"That was good thinking," said Dais. "Are you okay, the side of your face is really swollen?"

"An' my neck?"

"It's red."

"He tried to strangle me."

"Bastard."

Emma knelt down beside the bath. "'The rest of you seems alright'"

"What!"

And she scooped up a handful of suds, the ones that were covering my cock.

"Emma," said Dais, "that is so naughty," and she giggled.

And Emma giggled. And then they left me steaming again.

My life was becoming so fucking manic.

Chapter 17

The sisters decided to go and get some more things for the house, curtains, sleeping bags, things like that. I went to Rowhedge to collect my cash.

Before I left I had shared my plan about tailing Deer.

"Why him?"

"Cos he's a creepy fuck. He hangs around too much for it to be natural. I thought it'd be a good place to start."

"You got a Facebook page?"

"No, have you?"

"Yeah… both of us, and we can't use because we've run away and need to keep a low profile."

I wondered if Josh could be found by using Facebook.

"We could open a page in your name and start asking questions. We'll start tonight. We'll also help you follow that bloke."

I warned them about walking through the park during school hours, about how Boudicca's squads hunted kids down and marched them back to school. Things could get tricky if they allowed themselves to be questioned.

I'd never had a hobby, you know, something you could really get stuck into, so the single mindedness of trying to find my kidnapped brother galvanised me like I'd never been galvanised before. The hunt for Josh consumed me and most of my thoughts, kept me focused. And only things like scantily dressed sisters distracted me, but, I figured, scantily dressed sisters would distract anyone.

The cash was still where I'd left it, which, along with Josh's picture and the garlic, went inside my jacket. I rolled up the duvet and placed it in a big plastic bag with the other stuff that had made the place feel like a home for the night, and stashed it under cover, just in case. I was back at the park by lunch-time. I set myself up at the clump.

Just as it had done for the past week, the sun shone, and the workers and students spilled out onto the grassy slopes. Two women pushing invalids in wheelchairs were struggling up the twisting pathway… and behind them was the castle gang. They were all there… Mo, Stick, Fallon, Lee, Franny and Spider. The only one missing was me. They were obviously making comments of some sort about the women, because they were laughing and the women were obviously taking offence.

They turned to face the group and one angrily shouted. "You lot should stop taking the piss and help us… or get back to school." They were very brave.

"Ooh, listen to the fat cow."

I must admit Spider had got it spot on. All the same, it was a mistake for the woman to be confrontational. They should have just stood aside and swallowed their pride, the gang would have probably left them alone.

"Let's help you then madam." Lee shoved one of the pushers aside and took control of the wheelchair. Franny grabbed the other one and both then started to race up the hill. The men being pushed were retarded and started screaming and howling with fright. That made things worse for them and funnier for the gang. I wanted to go and put a stop to it. I wished I could.

The two women carers chased after the wheelchairs and Mo, Fallon and Spider ran amongst them, abusing and obstructing them and making life difficult. Stick just stayed where he was, puffing away on a cigarette. It seemed as though he wanted nothing to do with it all.

As Lee and Franny reached the brow of the hill a group of five college students, two guys and three girls, barred their way.

"Leave them alone, you arseholes."

Lee came to a halt, "Who the fuckin hell are you talking to?"

"Not in the top class at school then?"

I could hardly bare to watch. Lee stepped forward towards the mouthy blond bloke, and the next thing I knew, Lee was on the floor, felled by the fastest right hook I'd ever seen. Franny was rooted to the spot, bewildered. He even allowed one of the girls in the group to snatch his wheelchair. Another girl grabbed the other one.

By this time Mo and the others had caught up, but loads of other sun worshipers, buoyed by the blond guy's bravery, had gathered around to support the carers. I thought there was going to be a fight, but the gang backed down and made a cowardly departure, Lee rubbing the side of his face as ridicule and abuse rained down on them. Stick hadn't become involved, he'd just stood and watched the whole episode. Then he stubbed out his fag with a swivelling foot, turned, and walked away in the opposite direction.

Two community police turned up. Somebody had dialled 999 when the fracas began, and, after a few minutes of talking to bystanders they escorted the carers and their patients as they continued on their journey.

The whole affair was puky. Made me glad that I no longer hung with the gang… I was embarrassed by their antics. But, what about Stick? Did he feel the same way?

The park calmed down. As the afternoon approached most of sun seekers disappeared, and out came Boudicca's Angels. Within half an hour they had stopped two people, both men, chatted, and then the

114

men continued on their way. The next one was a small girl, I initially thought about my age. But she produced something from a shoulder-bag, a driver's licence perhaps, and they allowed her to pass through. The next one was interesting though.

Male. Twenty-ish. He was obviously very down on his luck, the way he walked, and he was scruffy, dirty. Three women began a conversation with him. If there had been a signal I didn't see it. The other group waddled over and soon the bloke was surrounded by seven eager women. They looked to be speaking to him in a kindly manner, one even stroked his shoulder in a concerned way as he told them his story.

Then two of them walked off with him towards the bottom of the park, where a car waited, and he climbed in the back. I couldn't see from this distance who was in the vehicle, aside from the bloke who just got in, but there was obviously a driver because it drove off, and the women returned to patrol the park.

In the next hour they stopped six more people, two were led away, but not to any car I could see. Then *the* car returned… the one that had earlier been used to take away the scruffy bloke, and out of the driver's seat climbed Michael Deer. Even from that distance it was hard to mistake him… I could almost feel him. Anyway, he walked off, away from the park and towards the football ground.

I skirted around the edge of the park to avoid the Angels, and approached the car from alongside the rough piece of ground, which they kept for dogs to shit on. Its windows were dark and I couldn't see inside, so I had to be careful. As I walked alongside I keyed it for a reaction and a bloke jumped from the back seat.

"Oi! You little bastard."

I ran off, but not far. He didn't follow, just got back in the car. I made a mental note of the number. The car was old, an Audi. Again I walked towards it, much slower this time.

The bloke opened the door, stepped out and leaned against the vehicle. "What's your fuckin game you cunt?"

I stood and faced him, showing him it would take more than words to scare me off.

He lifted his right hand, smiled, and then fucking shot at me, with a fucking gun! I legged it! Fuck!

* * *

I watched the parked car from a safe distance for another half an hour. Deer returned. The bloke in the back got out and they talked and he pointed in my direction. Deer remonstrated with the guy, pushed him and waggled a finger. Then they both got back in and drove off.

I thought back to the first time I'd noticed one of the Angels' "lost souls" being driven off. I tried, but couldn't remember the car… it *could* have been the same one. But I didn't think it had been driven by Deer, I'm sure he was walking around the park canoodling with his mum and the rest of the Boudicca mob at the time. Still, I didn't let that little fact put me off. Michael Deer, queer, kidnapper!

Chapter 18

I knew where Deer lived. I hung around watching his house until after dark. He didn't show. By the time I'd called it a day and arrived home, it was past midnight.

The big bedroom had a sheet pinned up at the window. The sisters were tucked up and soundo in a large sleeping bag, and, on top of a blown-up mattress! Was I Jealous? The pile of cases had been emptied and pushed over to the side of the room.

They'd been shopping. The kitchen had some bits and pieces on the worktops. I grabbed and downed a bowl of cereal. I studied them sleeping for a while, wanting so much to slide in beside them. They'd brought an extra pillow, which had been conveniently placed on the other side of the room. I wanted to crawl into their bag, had I mentioned that already? I noisily washed, hoping to arouse them, but the only one aroused was me, although I was sure I heard a tiny giggle as I slipped off to sleep.

Day 9 Friday

I've heard it said that most of your dreams are dreamt just before you wake up, which isn't fair. I was dreaming of the two of them wandering around the house naked, and awoke to find them in the final stages of dressing! I pleaded with them to get undressed again.

"Pervert!"

"I need you… I could be dead soon."

"Wanker."

"I could be. I was shot at yesterday."

"No you weren't."

"Yes I was," and I told them all about it.

They were both clearly shocked. "What do you think is happening?"

I'd already given it some thought. "I don't know, perhaps nothing, perhaps they're just taking people to a halfway house or something."

"People who take people to halfway houses don't shoot at other people."

That's exactly what I thought. "That's what I thought."

"What about sex?"

"Make your mind up… you just said…"

"This is serious, stop playing around."

I had to try.

119

"That's one thing, sex." Dais was doing most of the talking. "Maybe they're driving vulnerable people off to somewhere quiet and having sex with them. The other is... they're kidnapping them."

"I'm inclined to think it's the sex thing."

"I would have thought that if it was for sex they'd have taken a girl, not a dirty tramp of a bloke."

"We're talking about Michael Deer, queer."

"How do you know he's gay?"

"Cos I do. Everybody knows."

"That's probably just talk, because of the way he looks and acts."

"It's not talk!"

Dais carried on as though she knew better, and everybody else was thick. "Why... have you seen him with another bloke then?"

I was quiet.

"See, you don't know. It happens all the time, somebody says something and suddenly it's fact. Ridiculous!"

I could have said it... blurted it out... He raped me! But I didn't. I let her carry on for a while, getting her point over, then went to the bathroom and dressed. I think she knew she'd upset me but we both let it go, I had more important things to do, like continue my investigation of Michael Deer.

I returned to my favourite spot in the park but, unlike the previous days, it was overcast, and by ten it was spitting with rain. There were no squads of Angels, no parked Audi and no Michael Deer so I decided to make my way down to his house and have a look round.

The house looked like any common semi-detached house that you found in small streets of big towns, all clumped close together with only enough space between for a shared single path into the back gardens. If the Audi belonged to Deer, it wasn't parked outside.

I edged my way along the path between Deer's place and his neighbour's. At the rear of the houses there were two tall solid wooden gates, angled entrances to the back yards. I gently tried Deer's. It was locked.

I slowly allowed the latch to drop back into place without making a noise. Just in time… I heard his back door being unlocked. It opened! He was on one side of the gate. I was on the other. He obviously went to a dustbin because I heard the lid being taken off. I held my breath and was ready to leg it. Whatever he was doing took ages, and twice he cleared his throat and gobbed. He was a noisy breather as well, he was disgusting! Then he went back into the house.

My heart was thumping. I tried the neighbour's gate, that was locked as well. I decided I'd made a big mistake. I needed get out of the place, fast. I made it half way back down the side of the house when the fucking front door opened… he was leaving the house… I was trapped.

I quickly made it back to the garden gates and tried to blend in against the flat wooden face, like a chameleon that doesn't change colour. The front door slammed. Deer stepped down onto the path, then towards the road… just a few steps. He stopped, as if he couldn't make his mind up whether to turn left or right. Please God. He turned left… then back ninety degrees and looked along the path… straight at me… stuck against the gate. He froze… like the horny red devil, as if waiting for something to click, then, instead of collapsing into a box smaller than his mass, he turned and walked away. Fuck! I collapsed.

Decision time! There was only one choice really… but I took the other one and climbed over the fence. I tried the back door… the idiot had left it unlocked… I went in. I hadn't any idea what I was looking for. I think I was hoping that whatever it was would just pop up and smack me around the head.

His house was quite neat, a bit smelly, but neat. The carpets were thick and everything looked modern, like off the telly. He had a proper phone. I thought there might be some incriminating phone numbers and addresses in a book in a drawer or something, but if there was, I couldn't find it.

Downstairs there was a kitchen and one big living room that had an open staircase. Upstairs there were three rooms, a toilet and a bathroom. The walls and the carpets were white! The smallest room was an office. The other two were bedrooms. I rooted through the office, on the desk and in the drawers, but again I didn't find anything. He had a desktop PC and I booted it up… it went straight onto his desktop, no password required. I messed around with it for a while, even tried to find his emails, but wasn't clever enough to open anything.

The big bedroom had the biggest bed I'd ever seen and was obviously the one he used, there were loads of clothes piled on the bed in the smaller room, and other clothes: suits, trousers, shirts and stuff like that hung on a clothes rail, which had wheels on. I tried a bright red silk dressing gown on and pranced around in front of the big mirrors in the big room, pretending to be him, when the front door opened.

I tried to hide under the bed but you couldn't get under it because it had big drawers. The first one I tried was empty. I just about fitted inside.

He wasn't alone, there was another bloke. They were downstairs rabbiting away, although I couldn't make out what they were saying. I was wondering whether I had time to get to the window and jump out… but you guessed it, they came upstairs.

"So what did he say?"

"He said we are taking too many risks." That was Deer, I knew his voice.

"But it's them who are piling on the pressure."

"I know. It'll be a shame if we can't manage it though, an extra thirty grand for nothing would be a nice little bonus."

"The schools break up for summer the end of next week, it won't be so easy after that."

"That's what he said, but I've been making contingency plans. I think we could do it without raising suspicion."

"Endolin Hall?"

"Precisely."

"You know, I knew you were up to something when you kept some of them back."

I hadn't a clue what they were on about. What I did know was one of them was standing right next to the bed while he spoke. He started to dial somebody on his mobile. If anybody phoned me… Fuck! I managed to pull mine out, to switch it off, but suddenly I couldn't remember if it played a little tune as it shut down. I started to panic… my mind went blank, but I shouldn't have worried… there's always something worse around the corner.

"Someone's fuckin been in here!" That was Deer. "Look, stuff's all over the place."

They both started wandering all over the house, muttering and swearing. Then they came back into the bedroom.

A mobile again, it was Deer. "Geezer, where are ya? … Get yerself over to my place, fast as yer can … Some shit's broken in … and, Geezer, bring the dogs!"

Chapter 19

About ten minutes went by as they checked around the house to see if there was anything missing. It seemed like an hour. Then Geezer turned up. I don't know what sort of dogs they were, but the way they bounded up the stairs… they were big.

"Wipe their fucking feet."

"Mindy, Mork. Come ere."

"Here's some kitchen towel. Right, tell Pete what you told me in the pub the other day."

"They're fuckin something else these two. Let em ave a sniff round an' then let em loose. They'll find the fucker as quick as you can say Bob's yer uncle… an' rip im to pieces."

"But whoever was here has long gone."

"It don't matter, if e's local, they'll find im, an' still rip im to pieces."

"That's what I like, that's what I like." That was Deer, all enthusiastic. He was standing right beside my drawer, his leg jiggling with excitement and making the floorboards vibrate… which was just as well, because it hid my trembling.

"Yeah look, let em loose for a few minutes, I can tell when they've got the scent. Then you tell em this…"

"What?"

"This ere, what I've got written down… it's Croatian for 'attack', but don't say it, whatever yer do, until they're ready."

"Okay," said Deer, "let's get started then."

The dogs were let loose and proceeded to sniff all over the house. But their main interest was the bedroom… and the bed. I could feel it rock as they sniffed and slobbered all over it and pressed against it. I almost shouted out in surrender. Whatever had happened to me in the past was nothing compared to what was about to happen to me now.

"Right… they're ready boys… Mork. Mindy."

I began to cry.

"Let me do it." It was Deer. "Give me the paper, let me give the order."

"Well… should be okay." And I could picture Geezer handing Deer the piece of paper.

I waited for the dreaded word…

"NAPASTI!"

Suddenly all hell broke loose. There was a maddening scream amidst a rage of growling and snarling.

"GET EM OFF!"

"Mork, Mindy leave."

"AAAARGH"

"Mork, Mork, Mindy, Mork. Bad dogs… Leave. Leave.

"FUCKING AAAARGH! GET EM OFF MEEEE…"

"Say it in Croatian!"

"What?"

"AAAAARGH!"

"Leave!"

There was a short passage of snarling and thumping and screaming and growling, then…"

"OSTAVITI! OSTAVITY!"

"AAAAARGH!"

"OSTAVITI! OSTAVITY! Mork, Mindy… OSTAVITI! OSTAVITY!"

"AAAAARGH… FUCKING OSTAVITI! OSTAVITY! OSTAVITI! OSTAVITY!"

The dogs must have finally understood that they shouldn't have been attacking Michael Deer, either that or they'd had enough of eating him. From what I could make out from where I was, there wasn't much of him left."

"Call 999."

"I'm dying."

"Are you okay?"

"No I fucking ain't, get out of my sight. When I get back… you're fucking dead. And your fucking dogs."

Grrrr.

"I'm calling 999," said the other bloke.

"No, don't. Take me to hospital, to casualty before I bleed to fucking death. Not you… fuck off I told you, out of my fucking sight. KEEP THOSE DOGS AWAY FROM ME."

And after some clumping and clanking and lots of swearing, shouting and yelping, the door slammed and there was silence. After a while I eased the drawer open and crept out. The white carpet was covered in blood, ruined. Shame.

I needed to get out of the place, fast… but not before I smashed the computer on the floor… and threw his clothes out of the window… and put a chair through the front of his telly. You get the picture, I trashed the place, couldn't help it.

*   *   *

I was suddenly conscious of the money I had with me. I don't know what brought the concern on, but I needed to figure out what I was going to do with it. As I passed the boating lake and crossed the river I thought about going to Rowhedge again, maybe I could find somewhere to hide it, but if not, at least it would give me time to think. So I started to walk the short distance alongside the river towards East Gates, to catch the mono rail. One of the laces on my trainers had come undone and as I bent down to retie it, I saw him.

He was a *homeless*, long, uncombed hair and dirty clothes. There were a lot of them in Colchester, but I'm sure I'd seen this one before. On top of that he had stopped and was rooting around in his bag. When I started walking again, so did he.

All along Riverside Walk there are benches where anybody can sit and relax… watch the world go by, so I sat on the next one I came to. Homeless walked right by and I studied him, and he looked uneasy as I did. He must have been suspicious of my motives because it wasn't sitting and relaxing weather; too wet.

I doubled back on myself, over the bridge at the boating lake and walked along the South Side towards Middleborough Bridge, where all the riverside cafés and restaurants are. Molly's was ideal. It had a cover over the outside tables to keep off the rain. As well as that, sitting there, I could see almost the whole length of the pathway, from the park to Middleborough Bridge. I ordered a coke and a chocolate sponge.

Chapter 20

So, what about this money? Thinking about it more… hiding it at the pits at Rowhedge was too far away, I might need to get it in a hurry. I decided to put it in a tin and bury it in the back garden.

Then I thought about the bit of conversation I'd overheard at Deer's. Endolin Hall, he had said. From the blood on the carpet it looked as though Fatso was going to be out of action for a while, so Endolin Hall might be worth investigating. I wondered where it was.

Hello… Homeless came into sight. I fucking knew he was following me. He couldn't have seen me come into the café because he walked straight past. I waited until he reached the steps up to the bridge and was about to follow when a hand landed on my shoulder… it was Stick

"Fuckin hell… you nearly gave me a heart attack."

"What yer doin?"

"Nothing… just havin a coke, you know."

He sat down opposite and sighed. "I'm bored."

I shrugged.

"Ain't you, then?"

"Not really, no."

"Why?"

"Cos I ain't." I remembered I hadn't spoken to him since Mo had belted me. "You alright?"

"Yeah. Why, shouldn't I be?"

"Yeah, course you should. It's just that… well, you know?"

"No, I don't fuckin know."

"Well… Mo."

"Oh, yeah. No, I'm okay. Mo's a dick-head."

I waited, hoping he'd explain what he meant. "You want a coke?" He nodded and I ordered one for him and another one for me.

"Mo don't like it cos you fucked Fallon."

"What? Everybody fucks Fallon."

"See, that's your problem. Go round shoutin things like that an' then you wonder why Mo' whacks yer."

"But it's true."

"I know… but you just don't say it. Not now anyway, now Mo an' Fallon are an item."

"I didn't know they were."

"Well they are."

"Fuck. Fallon."

"No… you can't. That's my point."

I laughed… and he laughed. Fuck, me and Stick… laughing. The cokes came.

"It's not the same, you know, the gang, since you left."

Hearing him say that I'd left somehow made it permanent. I felt a bit rejected.

"I think the gang's all gonna fall apart," he said, "I'm thinkin of leavin em as well."

"Really? What, cos of me?"

He didn't answer. After a while he asked, "What's yer plans?"

"I'm not going back to school, that's for certain."

"What, never?"

"Never, ever."

"They'll make yer."

"Fuck em."

This was *Stick language* and he warmed to it. "Yeah… why should you do somethin just cos they say yer should. It's supposed to be a free country. Have yer got a job, cos that's what yer need… to stop em sendin yer back."

"I'm startin my own business."

"Fuck… what doin?"

"Detective."

He laughed. Not just a snigger, he roared. "Fuckin brill. Really?" But, somehow, it didn't strike me as a piss-take laugh. It was a friend's laugh.

"Yeah," the happiness was contagious, "a detective. I'm thinkin about a business, called the Colchester Detective Agency."

"Cool… the CDA." He stopped laughing. "CDA don't sound right."

"No?"

"No CD… seedy. That's no good, gives out the wrong message. Perhaps the Essex Detective Agency, the EDA."

"Brill. Yeah… the EDA. E… D… A…"

Stick laid back and looked at me funny. "Are yer serious?"

"Well… I wasn't. I just thought of it. But it sounds cool."

"Sounds fuckin awesome."

"Thing is… I'm lookin for Josh."

"Yer brother. Still missin then?"

I nodded. It was him who told me that Josh had been arrested… should I have it out with him, for lying?

"Can I help yer?"

"You?"

"Yeah, me. Why not?"

"No, no why not! Course you can. Ain't you going back to school though?"

"Not now, now I've got a job."

I was confused.

"Workin for the EDA."

"Pay's crap."

"Trainee. Yer know how those bastard bosses take advantage of trainees."

"Bastards!"

"Yeah… bastards."

Aside from showing Fallon my bruised legs, this was as happy as I'd been for ages... and, of course, the sisters showing up… and the horny red devil. I suppose I live a happy life really. If you took away being raped and tortured and smacked around the head every few minutes, being thrown out of the castle gang and having your brother kidnapped and your parents disappear. Parents disappear? now should that come under happiness or unhappiness? Like Deer almost being ripped to shreds by monster dogs, does that come under good, or bad?

"I've had one fuckin hell of a week, Stick. Do you know a bloke called Geezer?"

"Yeah, with his Rottweilers, yeah, mate of me old man."

"Is he a friend then?"

"Any friend of me old man's no friend of mine."

That was good to hear. So I told him about my near miss a couple of hours ago.

"Why yer following Deer?"

"I saw him an' another bloke drive off with a homeless, after the Boudicca brigade had collared one in the park, an' then, when I got inquisitive, the other bloke took a shot at me."

"Yer kiddin."

"No. Anyway, to me, it looks as though Deer is involved in somethin dodgy."

"Too right. Who was the bloke who shot at yer, do yer know?"

I shook my head. "Never seen him before."

By the time I'd finished, Stick was well impressed, I could tell, he couldn't keep still.

"It's a shame Stick weren't with yer."

"Why?"

"Cos Deer would ave been dead, an' he wouldn't ave been able to call up Geezer."

"But the other bloke in the house, what about him?"

"What was his name?"

I recalled the conversation… "Pete… I think."

Stick sucked air… "Pete. Yeah, I reckon I know who that was. Sleazy fucker. I'd ave to take im from behind, I think. You've made yerself a nice little bunch of enemies there."

"Well, they don't know it was me in the house, do they."

"No, but the dogs might."

"Fuck. I never thought of that."

"Our first priority then, even before findin yer brother. Kill the dogs."

"We can't kill the dogs."

"We ave to. I don't know what yer worried about, they're not nice dogs. They're not like cute little poodles… or sausage dogs. They're killers. They have to die!"

"Maybe they'll have forgotten me."

"They've got yer smell up their noses. Even if you don't see em for years, you'll have forgotten all about em an' be walkin down the street, mindin yer own business, not on yer guard cos you *ave* forgotten, an'…" he slammed his fist down on the table, making me jump, "they'll fuckin ave yer… an' you'll be dead!"

I wasn't sure if that was true, but this was Stick, and what it boiled down to was… if I didn't get the dogs, Stick would probably get me, and if he didn't, then the dogs might. The odds were stacked up against me, that's for sure. "Alright. How do we do it?"

He thought about it. "Poison… on raw meat."

"Where do we get the poison to kill a dog?"

"Well, we don't have to kill em, just put em to sleep, then kill em."

This sounded complicated. I just wanted to find Josh. I was beginning to think that it had been a mistake involving Stick, he was too unstable.

Suddenly he jumped up. "Leave figuring out how to take care of the dogs to me, We'll meet up later, an' tonight we'll sort em out."

"An' what do I do?"

"What were you gonna do, when I turned up."

"Follow a homeless."

"Which one?"

"I don't know him. He just made me suspicious."

Stick nodded as though he understood. "Okay."

"Well, I can't now, cos he's long gone. Come round my house at eight, you can meet the sisters."

"Sisters?"

"Yeah." I'd forgotten I hadn't mentioned them. "Come round later an' you can meet em, an' I'll tell you about em tonight, when we go after Geezer's dogs."

"Cool." He thumped me on the upper arm, a *we're mates* gesture, and I watched him disappear towards the lower park, hood up to protect himself from the light rain.

I paid for the cokes and then decided to go back and grab the sisters and get a bite to eat. It was half past two.

Chapter 21

Emma was alone. "Where's Dais?"

"Gone out shopping again. She says there's so much to get, seeing that we're having to start from scratch."

That was a shame because I wanted to run the *kill the dogs* thing past her, she may have had a better idea. "Have you eaten yet?"

"No, waiting till she gets back."

"Do you fancy a McDonald's?"

"Dais said I shouldn't go out, not during school hours."

"I'm hungry though."

"I can do some toast, or eggs on toast, how about that?"

"That's cool. How long has she been gone?"

"Ages. And she's not answering her mobile."

"Is that normal?"

"No."

Emma did some really hard fried eggs on toast, but the snack took care of the hunger. Then we played cards and generally messed around. At five o'clock Dais still hadn't returned. Emma was getting worried, and while I was as well, I tried not to show my concern. My imagination pictured Deer driving off with Dais in the back of the car, however, as he was probably stuck on some hospital ward in agony (I hoped), that was unlikely.

"Come on." I grabbed Emma and made for the door. "Let's go and look for her."

"What if she comes home and finds us gone?"

I left a note, to phone me.

Emma said that she hadn't any idea where Dais had been heading, so we started with the town centre and worked our way outwards. By eight we'd trawled a large section of the town without luck.

Then the mobile rang, and my hopes jumped… but it was Stick.

He was waiting for us at the house. Once inside, he couldn't get over the fact that all the furniture had been taken. This was another story I had to tell him, another time. He had one for me though.

"Fuckin Deer's dead!"

"What?"

"Deer, an' Pete the sleaze. Found in their car in the hospital car park, both shot in the head."

"Fuck!" I couldn't believe it. "Shot. Fuck."

"Turn the telly on." Stick looked around for it. "Where's yer telly?"

"Gone, with the rest of the stuff."

"Who took it?"

"Charlie Farthin, I think."

"Shit. Is he an enemy too?"

"No, he's alright, he's looking after me."

"Fuck, I don't know what's worse, him lookin after yer or havin im as an enemy. Still. Back to Deer. A mate of mine says the hospital car park is swarmin with cops, an' I checked out his house on the way here… cops everywhere."

This was news I could do without. Apart from fingerprints everywhere, I'd pissed all over his bed. I wasn't going to mention that, it's embarrassing, but at the time it felt like the right thing to do. Now they'll find me through piss DNA and connect me with the crime. My imagination started to run away and I wondered if he'd washed his cock since last Friday… surely at least he'd done that!

Stick brought me back. "You alright? I thought you'd be pleased with the news."

"Yeah, you have no idea. But. The cops will find out I was in his house, an' then I'll be linked with the shootings."

"Course you fuckin won't. You've got an alibi, you were with me, an' the woman who served you at the café will back that up. You'll be okay."

"Yeah." I sighed, he was probably right. "I wonder why he was shot?"

"Plenty of people hated im... maybe it was Geezer, after all, he threatened to kill im and his dogs, you said so."

"Well, we've decided to kill the fuckers as well. We're gonna wake up with our brains blown out if we're not careful."

"We'll ave to be careful then, won't we."

Old Bob's words resurfaced... keep clear of that one, he's trouble. We went upstairs, into the back bedroom we were using to sleep in, and sat on the floor. Things were developing at lightening pace.

"Dais has disappeared."

"Who's Dais?"

"My sister."

Emma amazed me, she hadn't even cried. Maybe she didn't realise the consequences...

"So that's Dais, Josh, and yer dad and Rosie?"

"No. Dad and Rosie have run off because they owe Charlie Farthin money. I'll tell you about it later."

"Fuckin hell. You've got so much to tell me."

"I told yer, I've had one fuckin hell of a week. No, it's just Josh an' Dais. But now, with Deer an' Pete the sleaze being shot... the thing is, Stick, do you still want to help?"

"Fuckin right I do."

I was hoping that he was having second thoughts. "Okay." I told him just about everything that I thought was important, other than the rape of course.

"The Angels!" He laughed. "This is crazy man."

"It's not funny if they've got Dais," and finally, Emma started to cry.

"I was thinking," I said, "maybe we should go to the police."

"No!" It was Emma. "Please don't go to them, please."

"But Dais might be in trouble."

"But you'll find her. And you've got Stick to help as well. Please don't tell the police."

"Why?"

"Please." She begged us not to go, but wouldn't say why we shouldn't.

"Okay. We won't go to the police… at the moment."

"Good, anyway, I don't suppose they'd do anything about her yet, she ain't been disappeared long enough," said Stick. "Together, we're gonna find your brother, and your sister, and it'll be the beginning of the EDA."

"What's the EDA?" asked Emma.

"Don't worry. Look Em, go an' make some tea or something, me an' Stick ave some planning to do."

Chapter 22

"What is it?" I looked at the powder that Stick was shaking onto the two meat steaks.

"Cocaine."

"What... where did you get it?"

"I nicked it from me Dad's stash."

"Won't he know?"

"Probably, but it don't matter because I ain't never goin back."

"What will it do, to the dogs?"

"I don't know, not exactly, but it has to do somethin."

Geezer's place was a scrap metal yard, down the Hythe. It was well dark by the time we got there. The place had corrugated metal fencing at the front, and the back was up against a huge hill of dirt, and that had barbed wire strung all over it. All in all, a very welcoming place, full of old cars and tyres. Stick told me that Geezer lived on the premises in a dirty old caravan, and the dogs roamed around the site when the yard was closed.

There was a tree outside the fence at one end of the site, which, when you climbed it, you could see into the place, but you couldn't get in that way, you either walked in through the gates or scrambled over the metal perimeter.

The two pieces of meat had been well soaked and smothered in cocaine and we had pushed the powder into it as much as we could. First, we made sure that nobody was in the yard, just the dogs. Then I climbed the tree while Stick carefully lobbed the steaks over the fence. Then he joined me.

It wasn't long before the hounds spied us and bounded viciously and noisily in our direction... I thought they were going to wake the whole neighbourhood. They ran right past the two bits of beef. I kept looking at the caravan, waiting for lights to come on, but they didn't.

After a while one of them found the meat, and immediately the other one joined him. But they didn't eat it.

"Maybe they've been trained not to eat stuff that's been thrown over the fence."

"Could be."

"Look, they keep sniffing it an' walking away, then coming back for another sniff."

"They're tempted, the fuckers. They know they shouldn't... but can't keep away. You watch, I bet they'll weaken an' gulp it down."

First, it looked as though Stick was wrong. Both dogs wandered back to their little hut and disappeared inside. I don't know what happened in that hut, maybe they had a conference and came to a decision that the meat was too good to resist... because they flew back out at a hell of a speed, straight for the chops, and wolfed them down.

After that they just trotted around the yard, taking it in turns to lead. Me and Stick were getting bored and were about to climb down from our tree when their trot became a run. They got faster and faster. It got scary. As they ran they started jumping.

"Did you see that, that one did a summersault."

"No it didn't, did it?"

"Yeah, look, it did it again."

"Fuck."

Suddenly one of them crashed into a heap of metal and just laid still, it looked broken. The other one continued to run like fuck, didn't even stop to see what was wrong with its mate. It was going crazy now, and making weird noises as it ran... and ran. Then it did another of its summersault type jumps and landed on its back... and just laid there.

We waited for either of them to move, but they didn't.

"We need to go in an' check em out," said Stick.

145

I didn't fancy that, but didn't want to look weak. "Yeah, I suppose we should, but what if they're resting, an' get us?"

I could tell that Stick was just as scared of that as I was, the way he thought about what I said. The summersault one was up our end of the yard.

"I might be able to see if I get closer… stand next to the fence."

I interlocked my fingers together and he used my hands as a step and hauled himself up onto my shoulders. He was just able to see over the jagged edge. "Pass me a brick."

"I can't."

"Why?"

"Cos your standin on my shoulders."

He thought about this. "I can hang on, if you're quick."

It was my turn to think. I knew he wanted to throw the brick at the dogs, to see if they were faking death. I didn't want to be any part of it… we'd done enough wrong already. Maybe if I took my time finding a brick, the corrugated fence would cut off his hands.

"Come on… hurry up." He was jogging up and down with impatience… and hurting my shoulders.

Enough! I suddenly felt really sorry for what we'd just done and started to walk away.

"What yer fuckin doin?" He tried to balance on my shoulders before toppling forward, saving himself from smashing into the ground by clinging to the fence. He dropped down. "Idiot. I could easily ave cut me throat on the metal."

"Well, you didn't. Come on, let's get out of here."

As we stepped onto the roadway a cop car rolled past with a dirty looking bloke sitting behind two policemen. For some reason, he glared at us.

"Fuck... It's Geezer! In the cop car," hissed Stick.

He didn't have to say any more, we scarpered. I turned to look back... to see Geezer standing at the entrance to his scrap yard and staring at us as the cops drove off. He was in for one hell of a surprise.

"Did he recognise us?" We both came to a halt at the bottom of Hythe Hill, hands on knees and out of breath.

"Fuckin right he did. He did me, anyway. I told yer, he knows my old man."

Bollocks. It always gets worse. "Let's get off the main road. When he finds the dogs he'll be out looking for us."

We made our way back home using side streets and footpaths.

"Can I stay at your place tonight?"

"Yeah, I suppose so. Let's go and see if Dais has turned up."

She hadn't, and Emma was in a right state, crying. The police had knocked.

"What did they say?"

"I didn't answer the door."

The three of us sat in the back bedroom. "Things ain't looking good," I said.

The others didn't answer, they didn't have to.

Chapter 23

I had a strange feeling, nervous, not because of all the enemies we seemed to be making, but because of what I'd done to the dogs. Stick spoke a lot of crap and I needed to start standing up to him or I'd end up getting nowhere in my hunt for Josh, and now Dais. I needed to get shot of him... but how?

Guilt drained me, and when Emma snuggled up against my chest I soon dropped off to sleep. One good thing had happened since Dad and Rosie had gone, I was getting some decent sleep.

Day 10 Saturday

Emma woke me, yanked me from a weird and scary dream. I was dreaming about Dais, fretting... somehow I was more worried about her than about Josh, I always figured he could take care of himself, but Dais? Instinct warned me that she was in great danger; her beauty was not her friend. Emma was stroking my face. "We will find Dais, won't we?"

"Course we will." She'd been crying again and I stroked her hair, "Course we will."

Stick had gone, just a messy pile of blankets and crumpled crisp packets in the corner.

"What are we going to do first?"

I shrugged, "Have some breakfast."

"You know what I mean, about finding Dais."

"Well, I can't follow Deer anymore."

"That was horrible, what happened to him. I think Stick did it."

"Really." I hadn't considered that. "No, I don't think so, he was with me when it happened…" just about.

"I don't like him."

"He's hard, an' nasty, but I don't think he'd shoot anyone."

"I think he would."

"He's okay, just a bit weird. I think his dad knocks him about, he's not a very nice bloke."

"Really." I could tell that her feelings softened. "Maybe I shouldn't judge people so quickly."

"Maybe… but never trust him." Emma had got me thinking though. Although I'd said otherwise, I think Stick was the one person I knew who wouldn't think twice about shooting anybody, if he had a gun. If Deer had had his throat cut I'd be highly suspicious, even if Stick was with me when it happened.

We ate breakfast in silence, both deep in thought, then we got ready to go out. "There's an internet café on North Hill. We'll go there an' see if we can find out where Endolin Hall is."

"What's at Endolin Hall?"

"Well, I can't follow Michael Deer any more, but I heard one of em mention this place, so… might be nothing, but you never know, an' I got nothin else, other than keep an eye on the Boudicca ladies."

"We're never going to find her…" and she started to cry again.

It took about twenty minutes to walk to North Hill. On the way we exchanged mobile numbers. I gave her Stick's. As we passed a news agent's I noticed the headlines… *Two Shot in Gangland Killings*. I bought the paper, the 'Anglian'.

"Why do you think they've called it a gangland killing?"

"The way they were killed I suppose. It doesn't say why, or that it was Deer and Pete the sleaze who died."

We spent a while on a computer but found nothing about Endolin Hall.

"Are you sure they said Endolin?"

"Yeah."

"What's Colchester's library like?"

"Alright I suppose." I tried to remember what it looked like inside. "It's big."

"We could try there, the librarians might be able to search better than us."

So that's where we headed. We didn't find anything to begin with, but then one of the librarians said she was sure she recalled the name and phoned her dad. She was old, so her dad must have been ancient, but he couldn't have been senile because he remembered it. In Langham, next to the old air field, by the A12.

We found the spot, on Google maps. The building that, we figured, had been built on the land where Endolin Hall used to be was big. It was surrounded by a high wall and had big iron gates… the perfect place to keep kidnapped people.

"Why do you want to know about Endolin Hall?" asked one of the Librarians.

"It's a homework question, for school," I said.

"It's a pity there aren't more children like you, keen. Good luck."

"Thanks." We're gonna need it!" We left with loads of printed information. On the way back to the house we purchased a map of this part of the country. Stick was home when we arrived.

"So yer gonna stake this place out then?"

"That's the idea, have a look inside if I can."

"I can't come with yer."

That was good news, but I couldn't help myself, "What you doin then?"

"Goin into business on me own."

I thought he was going to go on about the EDA, Essex Detective Agency, yesterday's joke, and when I didn't push him for more information, he grabbed my arm and pulled me into the garden.

"I'm goin into the drugs business."

"What? Where're you gonna get the drugs?"

"Already got a load. Me old man got collared by the law this mornin, came round our place and raided it, but I'd already shifted it, just left enough to get im banged up."

"You grassed him?" I asked.

"Stick don't grass."

I bet he did. "Where're you keepin the stuff?"

He smiled.

"Not here you can't."

"Why fuckin not?"

"Cos the law's gonna be here soon, lookin for me. And cos when Charlie Farthin's blokes come round, they'd find it, for sure."

"Good point. Yeah, I'll find somewhere else, soon. Good thinkin."

Quick thinking. This bloke was dangerous.

"Look, before yer go," and he shoved his hand inside his jacket. "Where you're goin, yer might need this." He pulled out a gun!

"Fuckin hell Stick."

"It was me old man's." He handed it to me.

"But!"

"But nothin. It's a semi-automatic, holds ten bullets in the magazine." He showed me how to load it. "Remember three things... load, safety, fire."

"Load, safety, fire."

"Yeah, don't fire it though, not here."

I don't know what got into me. I took it. It felt good. I stroked it and liked how it felt, made me feel taller. I put it in the pocket that didn't have the money in. He gave me a handful of bullets as well. I was itching to try it out, to shoot it!

He slapped me on the arm, "Go for it, but don't show it to anybody, not even her," and he pointed into the house.

Chapter 24

Me and Emma took a cab to Langham. I got the driver to drop us just down the road from the Hall. The gates were locked and there was a sign stuck up on one of the brick posts - Private Property - Keep Out. The place looked empty, the windows were boarded up and the lawns and flower beds were well overgrown. We knew, from the internet, that the walls completely surrounded the building. On the right hand side was another house and garden, but on the left was just rough woodland.

"I'm gonna go over the wall."

"I'm coming as well."

"No, you keep a lookout from out here."

"No way. We'll both go into the garden, and then I'll hide and keep a lookout while you go into the house."

We slipped along the wall on the left until we found a good spot to climb over. We were soon in the gardens, unseen. The place was in a right state, it looked as though it might collapse at any moment. At the back we found a door, rotten enough to be forced open. Inside, the place stunk and all the dusty hanging cobwebs made the place double scary. Emma followed me in.

"I thought you were gonna stay outside, on lookout."

"I'm scared."

We crept through every room in the house. It had a cellar, which was even more smelly than the rest of the house, and it was soon obvious that this wasn't the place Deer was on about. There were definitely no kidnapped kids in here.

"What are we going to do now?"

"I don't know, but this is a dead end. Perhaps we should go back to keeping an eye on Boudicca's Angels. I'll have to figure out a way to follow them an' find out where they take their homeless."

"Now Michael Deer is dead, maybe they won't take anybody else."

"That's possible. But if we don't get anywhere soon, we'll have to go to the police."

Emma was thinking along the same lines.

"The trouble is," I said, "it can't be long before they find out I was in Deer's house, an' with him being shot like he was, I think I'm gonna be in trouble. I think you should go an' tell em about Dais, an' even Josh, an' I'll keep on doing my own thing."

"How will they know you were in the house?"

"Finger prints, DNA."

"If I go alone they'll just send me straight back home… to him."

"Report him."

"He'll kill me."

Fucking Dads… are there any good ones?

"Come on," I put my arm around her shoulders and led her out into the gardens. "Let's go home an' think about it."

As we scrambled back onto the road an old lady approached us, waving a walking stick. We looked a mess. "What are you little buggers doing? Breaking in, I saw you." She was really aggressive.

"No." I said. "We're on a school project. We had to find out about Endolin Hall."

"Endolin Hall? Then what are you doing here?"

Stupid bag. I held my palms up, turned to look at the gates and pointed. "Cos this is Endolin Hall, or used to be."

"Never. This used to be Endeavour House. Who told you it was… what did you call it? Endo…"

"Endolin."

She violently shook her head. "No. Never. Endeavour House! Now get away from here or I'll call the police. If there's any vandalism been done I'll remember what you look like. Now bugger off!"

When we got back to town we checked home, just in case Dais was there. Then wandered the town, just in case she might be there. We were getting nowhere. We sat down at the monument at the top of the park, close by *those* toilets. We were both pretty dejected. Emma cried again. I didn't know what to say, to do. I put my arm around her shoulder and pulled her into me.

I'd never met Charlie Farthin, or seen a picture of him, so how did I know it was him? But I knew. He was massive. He was walking with Sitting Thug, and, as big as the sitting thug was, he was a dwarf compared to Farthin.

They greeted us like old friends.

"Hello Mista Farthin." That was the correct thing to say, I could tell by the pleased look on ST's face.

"Well hello boy," he growled, "I've been looking forward to meeting you ever since Gilbert told me about you."

Gilbert! Nice name. I almost laughed.

"So, what you kids been up to?" asked Charlie.

"Looking for my brother."

"Oh yes. Gilbert mentioned him. Still disappeared? Funny thing that, you're looking for your little brother and we're looking for your Dad and Mum. Perhaps we should join forces."

I didn't know if he was joking. "I don't know if I could help you with my Dad."

Charlie looked displeased.

"Cos I don't know where they've gone, if I did know, I'd tell you."

That pleased him. "I'll tell you what, boy, come to the club later, about seven, before the punters start to arrive. We'll have something to eat, get to know one another a little better, and perhaps we might be able to find something out."

It sounded like an invite, although I didn't think I had any other choice than to accept, so I accepted.

As Farthin turned and began to walk away, I asked ST where the club was.

"I'll pick ya up, just before seven… an' don't bring the girl." And he shoved a handful of notes into my hand as he spoke. "Wear something decent."

"I can't, you took all my stuff."

"Then buy something."

"Okay Gilbert." He saw I had a smirk on my face.

"Don't get cocky… " and clipped me around the ear.

"Who was that fat man?" asked Emma.

"Charlie Farthin. That was Charlie Farthin, the man himself."

When we got home I hid the gun and money in the shed, then I went into town and bought some new gear; jeans and tee shirt and stuff, good old Gilbert had given me another hundred quid.

Just as he'd said he would, Gilbert turned up at the house at quarter to seven, in a van. I hadn't thought about what sort of car he was going to use to collect me, but I didn't expect a dirty old van!

"I know what yer thinkin," he said as I climbed in, "but yer need to keep a low profile in our game."

I wondered what his game was.

"Do yer like Chinese?" he asked.

"Don't know any."

"Pratt. I mean food."

"Err, I don't know, never tried it."

"Yer joking, yer must have had it."

"I might have, but I can't remember."

"Well… fuck me. Anyway, we're having Chinese food. I'm sure yer'll be okay with it. I'll need to teach yer how to use chop-sticks."

"What, them little bits of wood?"

"Yeah, them little bits of wood."

I suddenly felt nervous. I was starving on account of me not eating because of tonight, and now he tells me I have to use those fucking thingy whatsit chop-sticks. I had a feeling I was being set up as the entertainment.

"I was only joking. Yer'll be able to use a fork… Charlie does. His fingers are too fat to use the sticks."

So why did he fucking say it? Gilbert did all the talking: remember where we're going, I won't be

160

picking you up every time; don't go shouting your mouth off about tonight or about the club, that's important; speak when you're spoken to; if Charlie likes you, you'll be alright.

"What if he don't like me?"

"He'll like yer, don't worry."

Chapter 25

We drove around and talked a bit. Then he doubled back and ended up in our part of town, don't ask me why, and parked in Dig Street. I could have walked and got there in five minutes…

The club didn't have a name, which was weird. He knocked on a shabby old brown door, and a bloke who looked like Gilbert opened it. Inside, to start with, it was a bit pokey, but then it opened up into the reception, where I left my jacket. I got a cloakroom ticket from a young bloke wearing a white shirt and tight black jeans. There's a lot to tell about the place and the people in it.

First, the people. There seemed to be four sorts: Charlie, a handful of Gilbert look-alikes, loads of young blokes all wearing white shirts and tight black jeans, they just stood around waiting for some command or other from Charlie or the Gilberts, and me. But, all blokes, you know, no girls.

Then, the club. It was well posh, all leather, dark wood and thick carpets. The first impression was that it was small, but the more I looked around, I realised that it was, in fact, the dead opposite; huge. There were lots of small areas around corners, hidden spots. I noticed... no mirrors. At the far end from where I entered there was a bar and a small dance-floor. The lighting was low and I was seated at a round table with Charlie, Gilbert and three other Gilberts.

"How are you then, boy?" asked Charlie, "you found us then?"

I laughed a little laugh. "Yeah," and nodded.

"We're having Chinese tonight, you like Chinese?"

I did answer, but was ignored. He turned his attention to the Gilberts, going over who was coming tonight, keep an eye on so-an-so, somebody else is not meeting the targets, some very special client who was bringing some important guests. But I didn't take any of it in, I was awestruck with the plush surroundings. I'd never seen anything like it before, anywhere.

I watched the young blokes. Some served our table, me included, with drinks on silver trays. Then they came with the food. First, big plates with dumplings and ginger, and bits of toast with seeds stuck on them and dippy things. All well tasty, I could have eaten loads more. Then we were given small bowls, and we helped ourselves to rice and sizzling meats in sauce and un-sizzling different meats in other sauces. Charlie and the Gilberts laughed and joked and watched me eat. Other young blokes checked this and that, pumped up cushions and cleaned the bar. Although everything seemed relaxed, everybody was doing something.

They said I was drinking champagne and it was making me giggle and burp then, all of a sudden, Charlie changed the subject. "Right boy, what about your brother?"

I'd forgotten why I was there.

"You got a photograph?"

I pulled out the only picture of Josh I had… and reluctantly handed it to him. The big man looked at it for a moment, and then passed it around the table.

He shook his head, "Don't say I recognise him."

All the others said the same as the photo passed by them.

"And now my friend has gone as well. Dais."

"Days?"

"Yeah, Dais… Daisy. She's disappeared as well."

"Perhaps they've run off together," said one of the other Gilberts, "you know, yer brother an' yer girlfriend… it happens," and they laughed.

I sneered, which, when you considered who I was with, was a pretty fucking stupid thing to do. Fortunately, Charlie seemed to be on my side.

"Shut it Gaz. Leave the kid alone." He shifted his attention back to me. "How long's your brother been gone?"

"Since last Saturday."

"And… Dais?"

"Since yesterday."

"Have you got a photo of her?"

I shook my head. "Not with me, I can get one."

"Can I have this one, what's his name?"

"Josh… It's the only one I've got."

"We'll copy it." Gaz, go and make a copy."

Gaz looked at it. "How do I do that?"

Charlie sighed. "Give it here," and he stood and walked off, picture in hand. I watched him. Strange though, he went into the gent's toilet. Funny place to have a copier.

He returned, he hadn't been long. "Sorted," and handed me Josh's picture… it was wet! I slid it back into my pocket.

"Now," continued Charlie, "my boys, Gilbert, who you know well, and Gaz, Phil and Mickey, will help you find your brother and your girlfriend. All you need to do is let us know if you hear anything, keep us informed of any developments, and we'll do our bit."

I was going to ask them about Endolin Hall, but now that he'd pissed on Josh's picture he could go to hell, I didn't need his help or the help of his thugs. Then I puked.

The next thing I knew I woke up in an office next to the kitchen. It was a big, noisy place, with other sorts of blokes scurrying about, wearing checked blue trousers and thick dirty white shirts. Smiling at me was a kid, about same age as me. He was also wearing kitchen gear.

"Fucking right one you are," he said.

I realised he was talking to me. "Wh… where am I."

"In the kitchens. Gilbert brought you down. Told me, when you come around, to show you the place, before you go home."

My head was spinning. "Show me around?"

"Yeah, see if you fancy working here, he said." Still smiling, he stuck out a hand, "Dek. I'm Dek."

This was too much. I closed my eyes again. Everything was spinning and it took will power and controlled breathing to stop it. When I calmed down and opened my eyes, Dek was still there, although this time he was sitting beside me.

"You alright?" and he handed me a glass of water.

I'd felt crap, but not as bad as I had earlier. "I think I'm okay, thanks." I thought about what had happened at the table. "I remember being sick."

"Don't worry about it. This is a club, people get pissed all the time, you're not the first to throw up, and you won't be the last."

That made me feel a bit better. He seemed like a nice kid, Dek. Good looking as well. There was shouting and clanging and lots of activity going on in the kitchen. "What time is it?"

"Ten."

"Are you supposed to be working?"

"I am working, looking after you. *You're* my job for the night. So, how come you're here… where're you from?"

"Castle Street."

He shrugged. "Town?"

"Colchester."

"Fuck, no. Colchester! You live here, in this town?"

"Yeah, what's wrong with that?"

"Nothing's wrong… it's just that you're the first person I've met here who comes from here. Most come from London, or Newcastle, or Manchester, in fact anywhere other than Colchester."

He was okay, very friendly, and I asked what he did, his job.

"Mostly I work in the kitchen, cleaning, fetching, stuff like that. That's until I'm sixteen, then I go upstairs."

"Upstairs?"

"Yeah, in the bar area, waiting… and other stuff."

I'd seen them. I knew what he meant, or I thought I did. "Can't you work up there when you're fifteen?"

"Do you know what sort of club this is?"

I shrugged.

"It's a gay club."

It didn't shock me, I just didn't know what to say.

"So, when you work up there, you're there to please the clients, anything and everything they want."

My imagination kicked in. "What, everything a gay bloke wants?" I thought of Michael Deer, and I wondered what sort of job I would do if I worked here. And I wondered if Charlie Farthin was gay... and Gilbert. "How many people work here?"

"It varies. Tonight, because it's a Saturday, there'll be a full house, especially as the Russian is here with some of his guests. Six in the kitchens, about five or six security and about thirty boys."

"Thirty?"

"Yeah, maybe even more. Although you *can* have too many, says Gilbert... pushes the prices down."

"Prices?"

Dek took a long hard look at me. "You don't know much, do you?"

I must admit I was a bit lost.

"This is a gay club. Blokes with money come here to relax and drink and dance. Some come with friends, others come alone. If they're alone there's always somebody to talk to... or to dance with. There are also rooms at the top, if one of them wants to take a boy for..." he shrugged, "anything. But they have to pay for that, lots."

"What, like they're prostitutes."

"Yeah, they call them rent boys though."

"And that's what you're gonna do?" I couldn't believe he would admit to it.

"Yeah, why not. Loads of money, if you're good at it."

"I'd rather earn it doing something else."

"You say that. Do you know that most of the boys earn the best part of a grand a week, where're you going to earn that sort of money?"

I shrugged. "Footballer, singer, banker, doctor. Teacher."

"And which one are you going to be?"

I didn't care. But I wasn't going to do that! Dek made us both a coffee and told me all about the work in the kitchens. He earned about two hundred a week, although he had to pay keep out of that. What he had over, Charlie looked after for him. He also said it would be nice if I worked here with him, better company than the cooks, they're all foreign. He said that Charlie didn't allow boys under sixteen to work the floor, and he told me that I could work here until I was sixteen and then leave, if that's what I wanted. Actually, that wasn't a bad option, worth consideration.

"How did you get this job?"

"I'm an orphan. I was at a kid's home in Peterborough and, one day, a couple of guys turned up and brought me to Colchester. They looked official and the manager was in on it, but I don't think it was legal,

169

because of school and the rest. That was almost a year ago."

"You didn't have a choice?"

Dek shrugged, "Suppose not, things like that happen when you spend your life in institutions, it's pretty normal."

"And what about the others, the boys. Was it the same with them?"

I didn't mean anything with these questions, just making conversation, but Dek looked a little uneasy, and hesitated before he continued. "The boys… yeah, with some it happened like that. Others are picked from the street. I don't know about all of them. As far as I know though, just about everybody is better off here than where they were." I waited for him to continue, but he changed the subject. "Gilbert tells me you're looking for your brother."

"Yeah. My younger brother, Josh. He's gone missing, no trace, and I've been trying to track him down. Charlie said he'd help. I've sort of come to a dead end. I was in the park watching groups of Boudicca's Angels approach kids, and some were taken off."

Dek butted in. "I know about them, they're just a group of women trying to help out."

"But they were working with a bloke called Michael Deer. I saw one 'down-an-out' driven off by him and his mate after the women had handed him over."

"Well, I don't know anything about him. As far as I know, everyone who's had anything to do with the women has turned out fine."

This news didn't make sense. "When I tried to check Deer's car, his mate shot at me."

"Really. Fuck. I must admit that doesn't sound kosher."

"No, that's what I thought."

"So, why don't you follow that up?"

"I can't. Deer and his mate are dead, shot."

"Are they the two blokes who got it in the hospital car park yesterday?"

"The same."

Dek whistled. "You need to be careful mate."

"I need to find my brother."

"Can't you go the police?"

"Not really, there are reasons why I can't involve them."

"But you need to find your brother, that must be the most important thing of all."

"Have you heard of a place called Endolin Hall?"

Dek thought about this, paced backwards and forwards across the office floor. "Don't think so... but the name does sound familiar. Why?"

"Cos I want to check it out."

"Why?"

"Deer mentioned it, I overheard him talking about it."

"Are you coming back tomorrow?"

I didn't know.

"Well, if you decide to work here, you'll be back. If not, call at the back door and ask for me. I'll ask around tomorrow, during the day, see if any of the boys have heard of it."

Dek showed me around as much as he could. The place was, by this time, extremely busy, even the rooms at the top. I tried to be enthusiastic about it all, ask questions, etcetera, but I still felt shitty, and a bit drunk. He showed me where the back door was and then took me to Gilbert, who was in reception.

"Well?" said Gilbert.

"Well what?"

"Do yer want a job?"

"In the kitchens?"

"No, as the fuckin manager. What do you think?"

"Yeah, alright."

"Start tomorrow?"

"Sure."

He arranged a cab. "Can yer find your own way here, about six-thirty?"

"Sure."

Chapter 26

Emma was asleep when I got home and Stick was nowhere to be seen. I fetched the money and the gun from the shed and put them back in my jacket, which stayed beside me all night. Emma was on the blow-up mattress and I snuggled up to her and dreamed about using Stick's gun... went through the motions, and then fell asleep.

Day 11 Sunday

Her stirring in the morning woke me. We laid together in silence for a while. She was nice and warm and I think I loved her... I kissed her on the forehead.

"Was last night alright?" She asked, "how did you get on?"

I told her all about it, apart from it being a gay club. I told her how they'd offered me a job and how Dek was going to try and find out about Endolin Hall.

"Did you ask them about Dais?"

"They asked for a photo, but I'm not sure we should show em, not yet. I don't know who to trust."

She didn't say any more, just laid there. I could feel her heart beating… and she was trembling slightly.

A while later we jumped up with a start when somebody came in the front door. But it was just Stick.

He emptied his pockets on the kitchen worktop. Notes, money, piles of crumpled up notes. He laughed. "Look at this lot. I think I've chosen the right line of business, don't you."

"What business?" asked Emma.

"Drugs." I said.

"Don't tell every fucker."

"Well, Emma should know, she lives here."

"Yeah, alright, but no one else, is that clear?"

Neither of us answered. If he didn't want anybody to know about his business, why tell us about it. I decided that I'd rather be a rent boy than a drug pusher, if it ever came down to having to make a choice. I think Stick was a little disappointed that we didn't ask about how he'd gone about selling the stuff as we ate breakfast and drank coffee. Anyway, after we'd eaten, he pulled me to one side.

"I've got somethin to tell yer. I haven't said before, because I knew you'd be upset, but yer need to know. The reason I've finished with the castle gang is… they were involved with Josh goin missin."

"What?"

174

"You heard me. They were involved. When I found out, I confronted em, an' they told me that I had to be part of the deal, or if I didn't want to be I could fuck off. So I fucked off."

"Why didn't you tell me earlier?" How could they do that? I felt my blood begin to boil.

"I told yer why, I was concerned about how yer'd react. But I was wrong, I should've told yer… If it was my brother they did it to, I'd kill em."

My brain went weird… everything went dark and flashes of coloured light made me want to scream out. Stick's face was distorted and his voice sounded muffled.

"You got the gun," he said.

Yeah, I had the gun. I threw on my jacket and stormed out of the house, leaving Emma open mouthed and Stick shouting encouragement.

Where would I find the bastards? How could Fallon or Mo be such shits. It was before nine so I went and waited down the road from her house, and the more I paced back and forth, the madder I became. I waited an hour, until she appeared… only one thought on my mind.

Looking back, at that moment I could have done a lot of harm. I'd lost it, completely. To be betrayed by your closest friends, people you'd grown up with… that would make anybody crazy.

I stayed out of sight until Fallon got to the bus stop at the end of the street. There was an alley, and I pushed her into it, I wanted to kill her.

"Bitch!"

She screamed.

"Stick told me."

"Stick told yer what? Get outa my fuckin face." She tried to fight me off but rage made me powerful.

"He told me about you and Josh."

"What about me and Josh?"

"Don't fuckin deny it. He told me how you an' Mo an' the others had something to do with Josh disappearin."

"We had nothin to do with it. You're fuckin mad. Stick told us you were accusin us... how could you, idiot. You're an arsehole. How could you think that? We're your mates, or were."

I was crying with rage, not listening to what she was saying. I wanted to kill her, right there. But I needed to know where Josh was. "Tell me where he is or I'll fuckin kill yer."

"I don't know. Why should I? Stick told us how you were shoutin yer mouth off, going around accusin us. Personally, at the time, I didn't believe him. But now."

"Stick told you what?"

"He told us what you was sayin… that's why we were mad with yer. That's why Mo hit yer."

"Stick told *me* that *you*… he told me that you an' Mo an' the others all had somethin to do with Josh disappearin… he said…" It didn't add up. Suddenly it did. I relaxed my grip and stepped away. "Fuck. Stick."

It was now Fallon's turn to lose it. She screamed in my face, "What the fuck are you playin at?" She started laying into me and I had to get physical, to stop her.

I stepped away from her blast. "Fallon," I screamed back.

"Get away from me!"

"Fallon. Fuckin shut up." She stopped her ranting. "Stick told me that you had somethin to do with Josh's disappearance. He told me that about an hour ago."

"What!" She was silent for a while. "Stick told us that you were sayin it days ago."

Suddenly, realisation. Stick was stirring it. "He wanted me to fuckin kill you. He's been manipulatin me… he gave me a gun, then told me that the gang, you, Mo, Lee, Spider an' Fran, had somethin to do with Josh goin. I could have shot you, I wanted to."

Fallon sat on the ground. "Mo hit you, because of what Stick said."

"Why did you throw Stick out of the gang?"

She shrugged. "It was nothin really, he was just throwing a tantrum, calling us all names. Mo told him to fuck off."

177

"You're not lying?"

She just looked at me. Then she pulled out her mobile and soon the others were with us. After what we had to tell them, they all agreed, Stick had gone too far.

Mo stepped forward and put his arms around me. "I'm so sorry man."

And they all said it, one after another. I almost cried.

They all wanted to see the gun, feel it. Admire it. Except Fallon. Why were girls always different?

Chapter 27

We all wandered into town after that, just like old times. It was crap. The only one who was interested in what was going on in my life was Fallon. The other four just wanted to walk around, kicking old tin cans and stones, talking about what they were going to do to Stick. I really had moved on. There was so much more to life than gangs. When we reached the High Street I decided to split. Mo, Lee, Spider and Fran didn't care, but Fallon wanted to be with me, she said. So much for Mo and Fallon being an item. There was a McDonald's in the High Street, not far from Bank Passage... that episode seemed an age ago… and we slipped off and got ourselves a coke.

"How's yer bruises?"

I laughed. "I got a job with im now, Charlie Farthin."

"Fuck, doin what?"

"Washing up and things, at his club."

"I didn't know he had a club."

That surprised me. "Josh's still missing, you know that. Well I teamed up with two sisters, Dais an' Emma, an' now the oldest one, Dais, has disappeared as well."

Fallon suddenly seemed a bit jealous. "How did that happen? The teaming up thing."

"I met em, an' they had some troubles that I helped em out with. Then they moved into my house. Rosie and Dad are still gone... gone for good I reckon."

Fallon didn't say anything.

"You'll have to meet em, you'll get on."

"That's if this Dais ever turns up again."

Bitch. There was no need to say that.

And she realised it. "Sorry, I didn't mean that. Course she'll turn up, so will Josh."

"The one bloke I suspected had something to do with it all was Michael Deer."

"Fuck, Deer...and Pete Blake. Poor fuckers, what a turn up."

"Poor fuckers, my arse. I watched the Boudicca squads in the park. They stop kids an' ask em if they're alright, homeless, etcetera, you know."

"Yeah, we've all seen em, fuckin old bags."

"Well, two of the kids they had stopped were driven off somewhere, the second time it was driven by Deer."

"So, that don't mean nothin."

"Maybe, but it looked sussy to me, and when I tried sneaking a look into the car, another bloke shot at me."

"What, with a gun?"

"What else? Anyway, at the time it was just Josh missing. I decided to follow Deer. At the same time Charlie Farthin's main thug, you know, the one who tortured me," I couldn't bring myself to name him, "came back and apologised for what he did an' that 'Mista Farthin' had found out that I didn't get on with Dad, an' wanted to make it up to me."

"What about Deer?"

"Friday was a big day. I started by breaking into his house, to see if I could find some evidence, but Deer an' Pete the sleaze, what's his name?"

"Blake."

"Came back an' nearly caught me. I hid under the bed, in a big drawer, an' they didn't find me. So they called this bloke called Geezer, he owns a scrap yard down the Hythe, an' he brought his Rottweilers with him, cos Deer knew somebody had been in the house but didn't know I was still there. They thought that the dogs would sniff the place all over, get my scent, you know, an' then go and find me."

Fallon had her hand over her mouth, it was sounding *really* scary... even to me.

"So they let em off an' they sniffed all over the house, especially the bed, an' then Geezer said they were ready. The command to attack was given, but they only fuckin attacked Deer! Nearly ripped the fat bastard to pieces, Geezer couldn't stop em. Fuck, was Deer mad! Told Geezer he was gonna kill him and his dogs, an' then Pete the sleaze took him to A & E."

"That's where they were shot."

"Yeah."

"Wasn't you who shot em then?"

"Course not. I was at his house. I'm not a maniac! Thing is though, I trashed the place, even pissed all over his bed."

"Don't blame you, I would have done the same."

"What, pissed on his bed?"

"Why not, girls piss as well."

Imagining that nearly tripped me up. "Anyway, the point is, Deer an' Pete have been shot, an' sooner or later the cops are gonna find my finger prints an' DNA all over his place, an' they're gonna be askin a lot of questions, an' I can't let that happen because I need to be lookin for Josh."

"And Dais."

"Yeah, an' now Dais as well. She disappeared after Deer was shot."

"So Deer wasn't involved?"

"I think he was, but obviously other people are as well. I overheard Deer talking about a place called Endolin Hall, heard of it?"

She shook her head. "Don't think so, I can ask around."

"Yeah, but be careful. I've been shot at, two kids are missing, two blokes have been murdered, an' two dogs are dead."

"Dogs! What, *the* dogs?"

"Yeah." I told her that story as well. And about Stick.

"Why do you think Stick is stirrin it?"

I thought about that. He manipulated me into helping kill the dogs, I'd figured that out. I think he just wanted to kill. "I think he tried to manipulate me, to kill you, because you'd pissed him off."

"Phew!" We both spent some time drinking the cokes and thinking about what I'd surmised. Stick was seriously deranged, we both agreed.

"And what about you, workin for Charlie Farthin?"

"That happened yesterday. We bumped into him at the top of the park, near the monument."

"We?"

"Me and Emma." I saw that look. "She's only thirteen, an' her sister's been snatched, we was lookin for clues, an' Endolin Hall. Charlie an' his bloke bumped into us an' started makin conversation. Then he said I should go to his club an' swap notes, he might be able to help me find Josh an' Dais an' I might be able to help him find my old man. So I went last night."

"Where's his club? I thought he sold second-hand cars."

"It's by the Dig Street car park, it's well hidden."

"Fuck, right under our noses."

"I had Chinese food with him an' four of his blokes, an' I was drinkin champagne an' ended up pukin. So they dumped me in the kitchens an' one of the workers took care of me."

"An' they offered you a job?"

"Yeah. In the kitchens, an' then, if I stay, when I'm sixteen I can work at the bar." That's as much as I was going to tell her. "Anyway, this guy who was lookin after me, Dek, he said he was gonna try an' find out about Endolin Hall, so I'm goin back tonight, to work an' to find out information, if I can."

"Didn't Charlie Farthin know anythin, surely if anybody did, it would be him."

"Maybe he does, maybe he doesn't, I don't trust him."

"You shouldn't trust his workers either."

"I know, I thought of that, but I need to find out, I have to take a chance."

"What did you say this bloke's name was?"

"Dek, why?"

"It's just that… if you go missin as well… I'm gonna take this to the police, so I need to know everything."

I thought about what I'd told her. I wasn't going tell her everything about the club, that was self-preservation. If Gilbert or Charlie found out I'd been shouting my mouth off I think I'd be in big trouble. There was no need to tell her that I might be gay. But I told her my theory about Josh, about Dad selling him to get money to pay back to Farthin.

"So if your dad owed Charlie Farthin money, Charlie Farthin would not have shoved cash through your front door."

"No, that's why I'm inclined to think Charlie's not involved with Josh, but I still don't entirely trust him."

"No, I think you're right, I wouldn't neither. What yer gonna do now, the rest of the day?"

I didn't know. I'd set out first thing to kill the castle gang... I wondered if Emma was okay. I went to the toilet and phoned her, told her that no one was dead and asked her if Stick was still there? No, he'd left, and she was okay, and how long was I going to be? I didn't know, I said. By twelve o'clock me and Fallon were at Rowhedge.

Chapter 28

I caught a glimpse of Homeless at Rowhedge Station, one moment he was there, the next, gone. I made a real effort to get sight of him again but there was nothing. Perhaps it wasn't him, after all, they all look the same.

We sat on the grass beside the river, warm under the midday sun, and continued our conversation about Stick.

"What yer gonna do about him?"

I didn't know. I was frightened of him, but didn't want to admit that to Fallon.

"And what about the gun?"

"I'm keepin that."

"That's stupid. What if it was the one used to shoot Deer?"

"I don't care. When I've found Josh an' Dais an' know they're alright, I'll get rid of it."

"Do you think Stick'll want it back?"

"Yeah, I suppose so. He's gone into the drugs business."

"Like his old man."

"His old man has been arrested an' Stick's got the drugs."

"Didn't know that, bout his old man. Fuck, I think we all need to steer clear of that nutter."

"The problem is, will he steer clear of us?"

It was nice, laying there in the sun, Fallon close, very close. I told her that I'd camped in the pits, and she wanted me to show her the exact spot.

I was on my back, right where I'd slept. Fallon was dancing a belly dancer's dance in front of me, her shirt undone and flapping, flashing her bra. It was nice. As she moved from side to side, her weight on one foot, then the other, she whispered, "There's a bloke watchin us."

I tensed up, but she shushed, it's okay, let him watch.

"What's he look like?"

"Dirty, long scruffy hair."

"Blue checked shirt?"

"Yeah."

"Fuckin Homeless. He's been followin me around."

"Really." She allowed her shirt to fall to the ground. "Well, if he fancied yer, he knows now that you're not gay."

"Yeah!"

She slipped her hands behind her back and her bra popped off. She laughed… she was playing to an audience of two now.

She whispered, "I bet he's playin with himself." She then stretched her arms up and back over her head, showing off her tits to the pervert, in fact any pervert who might be watching. That included me.

Homeless? He seemed to be very interested in me, and I'm sure it wasn't to watch me watching Fallon. I needed to speak to him.

"Do you think he can see me?"

"I don't think so." She ran her hands across her breasts as she spoke.

"Is he still there?"

"Yeah."

"Carry on prancin around, make him watch you. I'm gonna creep up on him while he's preoccupied. Where is he?"

"He's further along the path we walked along to get here, I've got my back to him."

She turned to face him and continued to run her hands over her body. I managed to drag my eyes from her arse and slid quietly up the steep sandy bank, under cover of the bushes. From the top I could see him, he was really lapping Fallon up. I crept towards him and slid down behind, further along the path, then I made my way carefully back towards him. He'd gone. Fuck.

Fallon appeared. "He must have seen you, or heard you. One minute he was there, the next, gone."

"Damn." She had pulled on her shirt.

By three o'clock we had arrived back at the house, just in time to see two policemen leading Emma away. They drove off with her in the back seat.

"Was that Emma?" asked Fallon.

"Yeah," I felt guilty, "if we'd been here this wouldn't have happened."

"No, if we'd been here we'd have been on our way to the cop-shop with her."

"That might be a good thing, perhaps we could tell em what's goin on."

"You can always go to the police later."

I decided that I shouldn't go back to the house, not to stay, anyway. I slipped in and collected what belongings I had. How much could I trust Fallon. That had never been an issue up till now, but there was no way I was going to take two and half thousand quid and a gun with me to the club, but could I leave it with her? I didn't have a choice.

"Where did you get all this cash?"

"I told you, that's what came through the door, as payment for Josh. You have to look after it for me, I might need it to buy him back."

She wrapped the money and the gun in a plastic bag and put it in another bag. "I'll keep it for you until tomorrow."

"Fallon. Watch out for Stick."

I got to the club at six-thirty and entered using the back door. I'd never felt like this before, like I was somebody special, the security guy greeted me like one of the gang. I went straight to the kitchens and found Dek. He'd got some kitchen gear for me to wear.

"Put it on," he said.

"How do you know my size?"

"I'm good at sizes… I bet it fits you perfectly." He helped me put it on. "You look fantastic." He tucked my shirt into my trousers, a little too personal, I thought. He then spun me around and brushed my shoulders and back and patted my behind.

I thought he was taking the piss.

Then he pulled out a bottle. Champaign again.

"Is this allowed?"

"Course it isn't." And he poured two glasses.

I looked out into the main kitchen.

"Don't worry about that lot. Come on, drink up. We're celebrating your new job."

Dek was persuasive but I didn't want to end up ill again, so I sipped slowly. Even so, it didn't take long for me to lighten up. He then went on to tell me what he'd found out about Endolin Hall.

"There's no such place, not officially. Endolin is sort of a play on words, for 'end of the line' hall. It's real name is Wylander House. It's on an old mental hospital site, Severalls."

"Severalls Hospital. Yeah, I know the place. I've played football there. It's like a small town, but for nutters."

Dek nodded. "It used to be. It's closed down now. But Wylander House used to be an entry ward for young people with mental problems. Apparently, they called it Endolin Hall because if you went in there it was generally the end of the line for you. After that, if you went anywhere, you went on into the main hospital"

"I want to go there."

"Go tomorrow, I'll come with you."

"No. I want to go now. Josh could be there."

"I don't think that'd be a good idea. Come on, wait until the morning, when it's light."

"It's still light now. We could get there an' check it out, before it gets dark."

Dek was quiet. "Gilbert won't let you leave, not till the end of the shift."

"He can't stop me."

"I think he could."

Of course he could. What was I thinking? It hadn't been that long ago when he was torturing me. I slumped back into the chair. "Would he stop me?"

"Yeah, I think so."

"I'll ask him if I can go."

Dek told me how he'd asked the boys discreetly about Endolin Hall, because he didn't really trust Charlie, or Gilbert, he'd heard stories. He said it might be a bad idea to let them in on what we'd found out. "Wait till tomorrow." He placed his hand on my knee. "Have you thought that Charlie might be being friendly so that he can keep an eye on what you are doing, so that he knows how successful your search for your brother is going?"

I considered this, and it made sense. I sipped my drink and watched Dek's hand. It didn't move. After half a minute I stood. "Okay, I'll wait until tomorrow."

Dek stood behind me, close, and assured me I was doing the right thing. I could feel his breath on my neck as he spoke.

Course. I should have realised he was gay, when he said he wanted to work upstairs. I tried to think of something to say, to put him off.

"I'm not gay Dek."

"Not yet you're not." He backed off.

"I never will be."

He shrugged. "Never say never."

I decided not to have any more to drink, and we went and started preparing for the evening. Dek showed me how to make small bread rolls, "We do this in small batches, all night long, a few here, a few there, making sure there are always enough in the proving ovens."

As the evening went on, we had pans, cutlery, crockery and glasses to wash. They were all done in dishwashers, we loaded them and unloaded them and then put them away. The evening flew by, until it was time to go home. Except, I didn't have a home to go to. I wondered what Dek's reaction would be if I asked him if I could sleep with him. I wasn't even tempted.

Chapter 29

The cab dropped me off at my house and I was tempted to go and kip inside but I knew that police often raided and arrested during the early hours of the morning, and that's what time it was. Rowhedge was out of the question, it was too late to get there. I nipped in quickly and grabbed a couple of blankets and then went to the bottom of the garden, under the hedge, and got myself as comfortable as I could and in a position where I could escape if I had to. It wasn't a good night.

Day 12 Monday

As the light started to replace darkness I shivered. Noise was sporadic, a cat here, a clang of a dustbin lid there. It was a semi-quietness I didn't particularly like... it was eerie.

I tried to relax but it was no good. Laying under the hedge was pointless, and I needed to pee. I'd made up my mind though, I wasn't going back into the house unless I was certain I was safe.

I checked my mobile for the time. Five-fifteen... God. I couldn't wait for Fallon, the money and the gun would have to stay with her for the time being, I decided to make for Severalls Hospital without them.

I arrived at the main gates at seven o'clock and then wandered the grounds looking for Wylander House, which I couldn't find. A big section seemed to be cordoned off with signs up warning of *building work in progress*, or *danger – heavy construction machinery*, and things like that, and that's where the place I was looking for was obviously situated.

There was nobody about and I managed to climb over the metal fence, hoping there wasn't a 'Mork and Mindy' waiting for me. Compared to the well managed part I'd just left, it was like being in a different country... the grass was all overgrown and all sorts of rubbish, including big chunks of rubble, was scattered everywhere. The first building I came to must have been what used to be the main part of the hospital. The paintwork was flaky and most of the windows broken, and everything I touched as I crept inside gave the impression it was about to fall over. There were long corridors, really long, covered with dust and cobwebs, but what was really good was there were still signs up, pointing the direction to various wards and things.

It was interesting. I passed all sorts of places. Apart from old wards, there was the hospital cinema, the café and the sports centre. Eventually I came to a big map of the whole complex, and right on the boundary, away from the main part that I was in, was Wylander House.

I worked out my bearings and homed in on my destination.

It didn't take long to find. It was massive, old fashioned. Built of red bricks.

I climbed to the top floor of the main hospital and was able to look down on the building, though there was still more than a hundred metres between me and its perimeter. Although it was in the grounds of the disued hospital, it was fenced off from the rest. I could just make out a lane that vehicles used to gain access, on the far side from where I was.

There didn't look anything particularly sinister about the place, there were even people walking about the grounds, it didn't look like it was some sort of secret establishment hiding imprisoned kidnapped kids. I wondered if I could get away with walking into the place… only one way to find out.

The main entrance was a double door, leading into an empty area, or room. This had no furniture. Even the walls were bare, although there were patches where pictures or signs used to be. The place could have done with one of those TV makeovers. There were two doors. One led into a fairly long, and empty, corridor, the other into a very large room with old un-matching sofas around the walls. Four kids sat on them. I entered.

At the far end of the room was a counter, or bar, and behind that, two doors. As I stepped into the room two men came through one of the doors and walked towards me… and straight past and continued out through the door I had come through.

I had my hands stuffed deep into my pockets, trying to look as though I was used to the place, and, rather than just stand, looking like a lemon, I wandered around the edge until I came to a sofa where one young kid sat alone. I plonked myself down, a couple of seats away, but close enough to speak.

"Hiya."

He looked up but didn't speak. He had the same look that Stick often wore but I doubted very much if he was as vicious. After a couple of minutes I began to feel uneasy, you know, embarrassed. I didn't know whether to have another attempt at making a connection or go an find another seat. Another youth, male and about my age, perhaps slightly younger, entered through the same door that the two men had earlier used. He scanned the room and then made a bee-line for me.

"Hi," and plonked himself down beside me. "If you're trying to strike up a conversation with that waster, forget it."

"Hi," I replied. "No, not really. Just sat down."

"You just got in?"

"Visiting."

"Right, that's a first, I think. Only been here three weeks myself, which isn't long, but it's a fair while for this place. Kids wiz in and out like I don't know what. Who you visiting?"

"I'm not actually visiting, I'm looking for two kids, one's my brother," I pulled out Josh's picture, which was now getting a bit worse for wear, "look," I showed him. "He's eleven… an' the other one's a girl, fifteen, blond, well dressed, you know, smart."

He looked at the photo. "No. I've not seen him. The girl though, she could be any one of a number of kids who come through. The older ones seem to be whisked through really quickly."

"She's not older, fifteen," I said.

"That's older for in here."

"But you might have seen her, it would have been during the last couple of days."

"Yeah, might have. Haven't you got her picture?"

"No. I'm gonna have to go an' pick one up."

"If you show me a picture I'll know for definite if she's been here."

The other kid, the one who I first spoke to, stood and walked off.

"What was wrong with him?"

"Dunno. He never talks, not to anyone. Just wanders around the place like a zombie."

"Is he a nutter?"

"Don't think so, why do you ask that?"

"Just this place, you know."

"No, I don't know."

"Well." I didn't know what to say, realising I'd said the wrong thing. "Apparently, this place used to be a mental hospital, years ago. It was a stupid connection, that, an' the way you described him."

"Well it ain't a mental hospital now, it's a charitable institution, a place for helping distressed kids."

"You don't strike me as distressed." I hoped that was a compliment.

"I'm not. I'm fourteen and an orphan, so it's the government's responsibility to take care of me, but I don't like the shitty homes they put us in, so I've ended up here."

"What's this place if it ain't a home then?" I asked him.

"Dunno exactly… half-way house I suppose. Nice place though, they treat you okay, not like most of the homes, the ones I've been in anyway. There's no Social Services for a start. They're arseholes, don't give a shit about anybody, they don't."

"How did you get here?"

"I bunked off from a home in Oxford."

"Why?"

"Because I wanted to. I told you, it was a shitty kid's home. You got parents?"

"Sort of. Step mum and bastard of a dad. They've fucked off though, so I suppose I haven't any more."

"But you've got parents, even if they don't care for you. If you ain't got parents you're like a dog, kicked from pillar to post. You belong to them… They beat you, fuck you, even sell you. They're all in it together… the councils, the managers… you're like their slave. I ran off because the manager wanted me to deliver some gear for him, you know, drugs. My mate ran for him and was picked up by the law, I don't know what's gonna happen to *him*."

He pulled up a coffee table, plonked his feet on it and slumped back into the chair. He continued. "Not here though. This place is alright. They seem to like you, care for you. Apparently they look for a family or someone who really wants to see you get on, to look after you and give you a decent start in life. Or even a job! That's what I've heard, anyway, and I've no reason to disbelieve them. They're charity workers you see, don't get paid, do it out of kindness. They look for kids down on their luck, and older kids too, some in their twenties even. They say they're here to point you in the right direction. So I don't reckon your brother or your friend would be here, because they've got a family."

Listening to his glowing report about the place was actually making me a little despondent. It was beginning to sound like another dead end. He was a bit smaller than me… dark hair and slightly dark skin. "You don't look English."

He laughed slightly. "I think I am, someone said once that my mum was Spanish, but who knows." He shrugged. "Got any money?"

"Yeah, some."

"Lend us a fiver."

I pushed my hand into my back pocket.

"No, not here. They don't like money changing hands. Let's walk outside."

So we upped and walked outside. There was a wooden table, like they have in pub gardens, and we sat at that. I handed him the fiver.

"I'll give it back."

"It don't matter. If I show you the photo of my friend, that'd be worth it."

"Yeah, get it and come back. I don't think I'm going anywhere."

I had a thought, "Give me your mobile number."

"Can't. They don't allow mobiles."

"Really. That's weird."

"Look, they're good to us in here, but they have rules."

I know he said they were good to him, but he seemed sad, all the same. Perhaps it was because he was an orphan… perhaps all orphans are sad. I gave him another fiver and told him he was okay. I'd come back and see him later, if I could get a photo.

Chapter 30

I left using the small road, which was the normal way to get in and out of Wylander House. The sun was already warm and I took off my jacket and slung it over my shoulder, slowly walking and thinking about what the kid had told me when a car approached. I stood on the verge to give it plenty of room to pass, and as it did I recognised it… the old Audi, the one that Deer had driven. Maybe this wasn't the dead end I'd been thinking it was.

I returned to the entrance of the property and could see the car parked at the front of the house, next to a police car. Perhaps I could hide in the back! But it was too late. A bloke came out, got in and whizzed past me. Although I didn't recognise him, seeing the car had raised my hopes again.

By this time it was half past nine. Fallon would have been at school, assuming she bothered to go. I tried her mobile… she answered.

I told her all about Wylander House and the Audi and we decided to meet up. First though, I wanted to see if there was a photo of Dais, which meant going back to the house, but what choice did I have? I caught a bus back into town.

I got off at Middleborough and hung around outside the newspaper shop, weighing up the dangers of going back to the house. I knew I had to get a photo, but getting picked up by the police wasn't a good option. I was facing the shop window, making out I was studying the local ads, when, of all people, Gilbert came from nowhere and stood beside me.

"Hello boy, we need to go for a ride."

"Hi... I can't."

"You ain't got no choice," and he led me to his car, which was parked on double yellows, not a cop in sight. They were probably all staking out my house. At least it wasn't the beat up old van. "Charlie's not a happy bunny."

I hadn't a clue what he was on about, but I was put out at having to go off with him; letting Fallon down and not being able to get the photo. "Couldn't we just stop at my place, I need a photo of Dais, you know Dais, she's missing, I told you about her."

"You won't need no photos where you're goin."

"Where're we going?"

"For a ride."

That was fucking stupid and it crossed my mind to tell him as much, but he didn't seem in the right mood. We drove towards Mersea and turned right towards Layer. We passed the hut where me and Fallon did it for the first time, the 'Friday Woods Nature Centre'. I smiled, thinking about it. Then he turned left, passed a pub... I can't remember the name. We drove for about a mile down a bumpy track... into the woods. By this time I was completely confused. Gilbert had never struck me as a nature lover, flowers or animals.

He stopped the car. "Come on, out."

He opened his door and stepped out of the car. So did I.

"Give me your phone."

Weird request. I handed it to him.

He beckoned me to follow him into the woods. I wondered if Charlie had a secret club here, buried underground... or it could be a marijuana farm... that was more likely. Anyway, I got carried away thinking along these lines and had overtaken him on our trek into the wilds.

Suddenly he told me to stop. When I looked around he was holding a gun, pointing it at me. "Sorry boy," he said.

"HEY, WHAT YER DOIN!"

We both turned towards the shout... it was Stick!

What the fuck was he doing here? I don't know what registered first, Stick falling down or Gilbert firing the gun, but before I knew what I was doing I'd made a dash for it... and Gilbert was firing at me.

"Stop! You little bastard. Stop."

No way. I zigzagged as I ran, as fast as I could, putting a fair distance between him and me. Still bullets whizzed past my head, I could hear them thwacking against the trees. Eventually they stopped, but I didn't. I reached a clearing and was at the top of a hill. From here I could just see Gilbert's car, parked at the edge of the track. I listened out for him. After a while I heard two more distant cracks of his gun, and then saw him walk towards his car, get in and drive off.

My next concern was Stick. I was reluctant to return... but what if he was hurt bad? I made my way back down the hill and through the woods, slowly... I found him right where he'd fallen.

"Stick," I whispered. "Stick, are you alright?" There was no movement. I crept over to him and shook him gently... "Stick." He was laying face down, and when I turned him over, his face was half missing. He was dead!

I didn't think about how he'd got there or what he was doing... just that he'd saved my life... and now he was dead. I couldn't tell you how long I sat there, maybe a few minutes, perhaps even an hour, I don't know. I'd let him drop back as he was when I found him, with his blown away face against the dirt, and for as long as I sat there I stared at his short and still neat, but matted with dried blood, brown hair. Even now, days later, I can't believe he's dead.

Flies were buzzing around his bloody wounds. There was blood on his thigh. That must have been where Gilbert had shot him first, the one that had downed him. After that, I imagine the bastard walked over and shot him in the head, maybe twice... I so much wanted to kill Gilbert... more than I had wanted Michael Deer dead. At that moment, even more than I wanted to find Josh and Dais. Stick had saved my life and he'd paid the ultimate price, and so Charlie Farthin's sitting thug had to also pay the ultimate price. And Farthin as well, but mostly Gilbert. As far as I was concerned he was a dead man walking. I took out my garlic and placed a piece inside Stick's mouth.

A mobile went off. I looked around. It was Stick's. I pulled it out of his jacket pocket but it stopped ringing before I could answer it. Mo. I didn't want to talk to anybody. I went through Stick's contact list... just the rest of the gang. That was sad... that's when I started to cry. Somebody had to know that Stick was dead, and that he died a hero. We needed to forget his strange ways... the castle gang was all he had, and we needed to remember him properly. I phoned Fallon.

"Hi... Stick?" she sounded surprised.

I told her it was me.

"What yer doin with Stick's mobile, and where the fuck are yer? I've been waiting for ages...and you're on the news."

I told her about Stick. "He saved my life Fallon."

She told me about me, how the police wanted to talk to me regarding the shootings of Michael Deer and Pete the sleaze.

After a lot of silences and a lot of questions she said she'd meet me at the Friday Woods Nature Centre.

Chapter 31

"Stick's dead, an' the bloke who killed him still wants to kill you. You're gonna be the next to get it, that's for sure. Go to the police, give yerself up… let them find Josh."

"What if they don't, what if they just arrest me for killin Deer an' throw away the key?"

Fallon didn't answer.

"Them fuckin Boudicca's Angels an' Michael Deer have been kidnappin loads of kids, I'm sure of it. Now it looks as though Charlie Farthin's involved. They've been using me, finding out how much I've managed to find out by pretendin to be my friends. If I give myself up to the cops, they'd probably believe me about Charlie, but if I accuse the Boudicca Angels, they'll think I'm mad."

"Where's Stick?" she asked.

We walked back to where he laid, and Fallon knelt down beside him, reached out and touched his head, and then said, "Kill the cunt."

It had been a bad move to go back to Stick.

If I'd been Gilbert I'd have waited, in hiding, waited for me to find Stick's body, then just coolly walk up behind me and shoot me in the back of the head, like he'd done Stick… problem solved, for him. He must have panicked and driven off. I knew, though, he'd be back.

"Fallon, we need to get out of here."

But she was all zombie-ish, in a daze.

"Fallon!" I tugged at her arm. She let me lead her back to the Nature Centre.

Just as I thought he would, Gilbert had realised his mistake. I was lucky, I saw him before he saw me. Fallon was still behind the hut, out of sight, when the car passed on its way back to where Stick was. And he wasn't alone… there were three other Gilberts with him. As I called out to Fallon, to get down, they saw me! In one move the brakes were slammed on and they all jumped out.

"Run." I shouted to Fallon… fortunately she did. I wanted them to follow me though, not her, so I ran, hell for leather, out onto the road and then into the field opposite. Running wasn't their strongest quality and I was outrunning the two that followed on foot. I decided not to bolt straight across the field, I needed all four to concentrate on me, including the other two who had gone back to collect the car. I was safely ahead of the two fatsos, but it didn't take long for the car to be alongside me, except on the road, on the other side of the hedge. Gilbert was sneering from the front, ready to kill again.

I expected them to shoot at me. The reason they didn't… a bloke was jogging on the path, right next to their car and between them and me. I expected them to shoot at him, and was getting ready to shout out a warning, but there was no sign of a gun and no shot rang out. The jogger was a squaddie, and he wasn't alone. Not far ahead must have been about twenty more, all running with huge back-packs on their backs, and rifles strapped on them. The Gilberts must have known they'd met their match, accepted defeat, angrily reversed, picked up the other two and drove off.

Ahead was a footpath that cut across the field, connecting Friday Woods to the army estates, and that's where the squaddies turned down. I decided to tag along. I couldn't exactly run amongst them, me being in jeans and hooded jacket, but I felt safer keeping close. I needed to try and think how the Gilberts might think. Would they drive around to the army area and wait for me? Probably. Using cunning would give me a better chance of getting out of this alive.

I rung Fallon using Stick's mobile. She was alright. I decided it was becoming too dangerous for anybody to hang with me. Fallon agreed. I told her to keep hold of the money and the gun and I made my way back towards the old mental hospital. Gilbert had tried to kill me, and the only thing that had changed since me being at the club was that I'd been snooping around Endolin

Hall, or its proper name, Wylander House. It must be dodgy, and, obviously, Farthin was involved.

I was convinced that following the Audi would lead me to Josh and Dais. The plan was to go back to the hospital and wait for it to turn up. On the way I dropped Stick's phone into a stream after first chucking the battery and SIM.

It was late afternoon by the time I got there. On the way, I'd plucked up the courage to slip into a Co-op and get some provisions... coke and crisps and stuff. I was completely on my own in the world now, not even a mobile to use. I thought about Emma, what had happened to her? I suppose they'd shipped her off, back home to her mum and the horrible Richard. She must have told the police about me, and Dais and Josh. She wouldn't have been able to keep any of it to herself, not the way the police interrogate people. Bastards. I wondered if that was why they wanted to speak to me, or was it my piss DNA they'd analysed?

I found a gap under the fence and wriggled through, into the other world that was the old hospital. In the section overlooking Wylander House, the place I'd found that morning, I set up camp. Lots of the windows were broken, but I found a room, probably once an office, with the glass still in place, so dirty no-one would have seen me through it from the outside. I pulled up an old chair with three legs, used bricks in place of the missing one, and made myself comfortable. I still had some garlic, I hoped there was enough.

Wylander House was quiet. I don't know what was over the other side but there were five cars parked where I could see, although not the Audi. I could easily see vehicles arriving and leaving. I was too far away to see faces, but a kid was wondering about in the sunshine… he looked like the zombie, but I couldn't be certain. What was interesting though, a couple of Gilberts seemed to be patrolling the perimeter.

There was nothing to do other than wait. I managed to close the door of the room and wedge a length of wood against it. It wouldn't keep out anyone out for long...

I waited. There *was* activity at Wylander House, normal routine stuff I suppose. A laundry van, seven or eight cars coming and going, people crossing the yard back and forth to a smaller building and, youths mostly, strolling around the grounds. I felt as though I'd been waiting ages, I'm sure I dropped off a couple of times, so I could have missed the Audi. What I hadn't bargained for, and should have, was Gilbert turning up with his mates. Stick had died because I had been snooping around Wylander House, their hunt for me would have obviously brought them back here. Fuck!

After they had all piled out of the car, Gilbert stood alone, legs apart and hands on hips. The other three were side by side leaning against the vehicle. All four were studying the ruined hospital, gazing in my direction. I could only guess what it was they were saying… *I bet the bastard's in that room over there!*

They began walking toward me.

I didn't hang around to collect my stuff, just legged it down the stairs, into the corridor... and ran. I had to make it around the first corner and out of sight before they got into the building. It was almost dark. Abandoned builder's equipment and other obstacles slowed me down, but I made it.

The old hospital was a massive site for four men to search... if I could find a good hiding place... Through the gloom I made out a doorway. It led to steps, down. I clung to the metal hand rail and carefully made my way, getting darker with each step. Even before I reached the bottom I couldn't see a thing. The steps stopped and the floor levelled. I prodded the air with a raised foot. The hand rail had ended when the steps ended. I was afraid to let go. What was down there... was it a dead end?

I wasn't in any doubt, if they caught me, they would kill me. My stomach churned. I lowered myself onto my hands and knees and slowly crawled, feeling my way by running the flats of my hands across the ground, in an arc. I think the floor was concrete, it was damp and cold and rough... and dirty. I could feel and smell the grime. Every now and then water dripped. I pulled my hood tighter over my head. As I slowly inched forward I knelt on a stone, or something hard and sharp, and was close to shouting out in agony.

I could hear voices but I couldn't tell if they were getting closer. I was in an underground corridor. One side had lots of pipes or thick cables running along the floor, the other side, about five feet across, had a gully with a metal grill. I was thinking that I'd be able to move faster standing and feeling my way, but even though my knees hurt, I felt safer staying down on them. I couldn't see a thing, not even my hands feeling the way in front of me. I should have kept Stick's mobile, I could have used it as a torch.

I crawled for a while, concentrating on not bumping into anything and listening out at the same time. The voices had faded, but just as scary was the silence that had replaced them. I stopped moving. The only sound now was my thumping heart and heavy breathing. A shuffle! A clunk on metal! I couldn't make out what the sounds were. Nothing again. A distant, muffled shout. Perhaps the noise was the Gilberts.

I gingerly stood, fighting my way through horrible thick cobwebs as I did so. Waving my arms, I couldn't feel anything else, like the ceiling. I took a step sideways, and could then touch things, pipes, big and small, and flat shelving, or metal tray, with more pipes, or perhaps cables, running along it. I edged my way across to the side above the gully, that felt clear. I wondered how many cobwebs it would take, wrapped around me, before I couldn't move, and lowered myself to the floor again... don't take unnecessary risks.

A squeak. Rats! I really didn't like this! Be brave, I told myself.

A dull light, from behind me, momentarily lighting up the corridor. Muffled voices.

"Look at this," a voice bounced along the walls.

214

"A service tunnel."

"E could be down ere... aaaah, fuck it. Cobwebs, everywhere."

"They would've been all broken if e'd come this way."

"Yeah, you're right. E ain't down ere."

Other mutterings and then silence again. Then more muttering, getting louder. Bangs, things being hit.

A shout. "Will you fuckin lot keep the noise down. Listen out for the little fucker."

They were definitely coming my way, but where were they? I was confused. They must have had those night lights, like the army use. They were walking along the tunnel towards me, and I couldn't see them. My heart sunk. They had me, no escaping. Some more talking, but I still couldn't see where they were or make out what they were saying, other than they were getting close. I could now make out footsteps. Then, a shaft of torch light, from above. There was a hole, a drain probably, from the main corridor into my tunnel. They all stopped, right above me. At least they weren't in the tunnel. I let out a sigh of relief. But if they looked down the hole! I kept dead still, fingers crossed.

"You two wait here. Me an' Gaz'll walk back round the main corridor an' search through all the old wards, see if we can flush im out. Keep yer noise down an' e'll hopefully run right inter yer."

"What do we do if e does?"

"Fuckin shoot the bastard. But make sure it's im first, don't fuckin shoot me or Gaz. An' turn that fuckin torch off."

Everything went quiet for a while, but I could tell two of them were still there, the odd cough and grunt... and one of them was jingling some keys. After a couple of minutes, one of them spoke.

"Why does Gil want this kid dead?"

"Dunno. Not exactly. I think e's been snoopin' around, an' the last thing we need at the moment is snoopy kids."

"At the moment?"

"Yeah, you know, what with Deer an' Pete Blake."

"Who had them killed?"

"Gill says it was the Tottenham Turks, they're makin' a play for our patch."

"That's why we're on high alert?"

"High alert, that's a good one. Yeah, we're on high alert cos the Turks are gettin greedy, that's what e says, anyway."

"Don't you think so?"

"No. Okay, the Turks are making a move. But I think Red ad im blown away. And Blake."

"I ain't met Red yet."

"E's the big boss, whatever Charlie says. E's also very discreet, keeps below the radar, if yer know what I mean. Deer was too ambitious, which is okay, but e was

216

also a fuckin loud mouth. So I think Red ad im seen to."

There was about half a minute of silence.

"What about this Russian?"

"Yea. And Lord Filf."

"Lord Filf. Who the fuck's Lord Filf?

"You know, Lord Filrothe."

"Oh..."

"It didn't help that Deer was makin waves, stirrin things when the Russian is visiting. An' I reckon that Lord Filf would fuckin run a mile at the first sign of publicity."

"What's Lord Filrothe got to do with anything?"

"Ain't yer seen im angin around?"

"No."

"E's a big player in the organisation, has lots of contacts, high up contacts. That means protection from the law an' newspaper people. If there was anythin that publicly linked im with Red or Charlie... or even with the Russian, e would cut those links, definite. An' even if it weren't public, if things got out about the kids, then e would cut the links, an' I reckon Red an' Charlie would be fucked, that's why this kid is a problem, e's found out too much, that's what I think."

"What has Lord Filrothe got to do with the kids?"

"Yer fuckin kidding me ain't yer. E's the biggest paedo out, likes em all, boys or girls, it don't matter, as

217

long as they're young enough. Charlie keeps im satisfied. An' his fuckin political mates, dirty bastards."

"Reall..." And a bunch of keys plopped onto the floor in front of me. "Fuck!"

I was frozen to the spot. Unable to move. A beam of light illuminated the area, me included.

"Shit, I've dropped the keys."

A head searched the area, using the torch.

"See anythin, what's down there, is it deep?"

"I don't know." The beam of light moved around, like a spot light, and stopped, right on my face. A couple of seconds, which seemed like an hour, passed. Then the spot light shifted onto the keys, laying in front of me. Then back onto me.

"It's okay," said the head at the hole. It's deep, but I can see the keys, on a ledge. I think I might be able to reach them."

What! Did he have a fucking rubber arm?

"If I stretch," and he shoved his arm down the hole and waggled his fingers. "I might, if I'm lucky, be able to get them."

The bloke was having a laugh. No way.

"If I can get them, we won't have to come down the hole!"

His hand was opening and closing, like a baby's who wants something... the penny dropped! I picked up the bunch of keys and placed them in the hand.

"Fucking got them!" and the hand withdrew.

"That was jammy."

"Fucking lucky," said the one with the hand.

I backed away from the hole, slowly. Far enough so that if anybody else looked down it they wouldn't see me. Why had this bloke not given me away? They were still talking, but I'd moved too far away to hear any more. One of Charlie's blokes was on *my* side. I had worked it out... he must be a Turk! A Tottenham Turk had infiltrated the gang. That would piss Charlie off, if he found out he had a mole who was a Tottenham Turk, and that the Turks were on my side. The big pity was, I couldn't make out what the bloke had looked like.

Chapter 32

I waited for ages. Every now and then a beam of light streaked down the hole. At times there were distant, angry shouts. Eventually though, it stayed dark and it stayed quiet. Funny thing, quiet. When a noise leaves, you think it's quiet… but it's not, it's just quiet enough to hear other noises, like rat noises.

I hate rats, especially when there are millions of them, like the ones that attacked Indiana Jones in those caves. This tunnel was like those caves. I was trying to relax, on my stomach, head resting on my arms, and eyes closed, thinking that if I dozed, the time would fly by faster. But it was too cold to sleep and was just about to stand and move about, warm myself up, when I heard them.

A squeak! I froze. Waiting. I think rats were already on my mind, but I didn't think I'd imagined it. I was flat on the floor, chin resting on the cold concrete and trying to see through the darkness. I put my ear to the cold floor. Could I hear the patter of feet? Could I? A sound… more… clicks and clanks like the central heating at home. But not rats. I was coming to the conclusion that I'd imagined it when something brushed against my nose.

I jumped up onto my feet like I'd never jumped up before and kicked out in all directions. I was more scared than when Gilbert first tortured me and even as much as when Deer cornered me in the toilets. I was screaming and shouting and, like an idiot, decided to make a run for it. Fortunately I smashed into the wall without all the pipes and cables on, but it still bloody hurt. I was shaking with fear as I slumped to the ground, then realised that I'd slumped back into danger and bounced straight back up, imagining thousands of them, swarming around me, preparing to leap and take chunks of flesh.

I'd completely lost it. The noise I made should have been heard by the whole of Colchester, but somehow or other I got away with it. The Gilberts hadn't heard me. I decided to make my way back towards the steps down into the tunnel, the way I had entered, by edging my way along the clear wall. The spider webs were still a problem, but not as big a one as the rats.

I'd been feeling my way along the wall until I decided that I'd gone too far... somehow or other I'd missed the steps! I felt my way across to the walls with the pipe work, and blindly made my way back towards where I'd started from. I had to be careful, there were loads of sharp edges waiting to rip my fingers. I gingerly felt my way, until the pipes turned away from me. This must be where the stairs were.

I bravely lowered myself to the floor, risking rat attacks, and used the ark method with my hand out in front of me to move forward… no steps! Think! I told myself. Stay calm. Where had I gone wrong? I was lost! What I did know was, that moving forward was wrong. I reversed until I touched the wall with my back side, back in the main tunnel.

When I first crawled along the tunnel I could have passed this corner without realising it. A feeling of dread spread through me, I might never get out of here. The worst thing was that I knew I would die a horrible death, eaten by the rats. I would pass out because of the cold, or thirst, or hunger… then I'd be eaten alive.

I wondered then, where Josh was. Was he as scared as I was? And what about Dais? They were both braver than me, and cleverer. If they were as scared as me, then they must be in big trouble. I had to get out of here… I was their only hope. I really had to get out of here! They were the thoughts that dominated me at that moment. Useless, stupid thoughts, instead of figuring out how to save myself. The only good thing was that thinking like that gave me a determination to survive. That crossed my mind at the time.

But… determination alone is not enough. I know I stood in that position for a long time, marvelling at how determined I'd become, but it wasn't until I began thinking that I could be too late to save them, that I eventually came to my senses. I carefully side stepped to my left, using the tray of pipe work as a guide, a waving hand feeling out for anything waiting to stab me in the head. An outstretched foot probing for hazards. I counted fifty steps, but found no way out. Fifty back to the starting point, then fifty to my right. Another fifty to the right. Still nothing. One hundred back, then another hundred left. By the time I had returned to my original starting point for the third time I was totally confused. The whole exercise had taken hours. I couldn't understand why I couldn't find the steps I'd entered the tunnel by.

Using the same method of travel, I slowly explored the offshoot from the main tunnel. Mostly it was dead quiet. Occasionally, and scarily, there would be a bang, which echoed through the whole system of tunnels. Each one might have come from a mile away, but each one frightened the life out of me. I hadn't a clue what the noises were. I lost count of my steps. I was freezing cold and shaking with fear. All I wanted to do was drop to the ground and sleep, but the thought of the rats kept me going. I spoke to Stick, thanking him for being my mate, asking him to guide me. I wondered *where* he would guide me… could I trust him! And then I worried that he might be able to hear my thoughts.

Every once in a while the pipes would tee off, generally upwards, but they also continued onwards. I was way, way past three, maybe four hundred side steps, and still the tunnel went on. Then, they changed direction, upwards. Not a tee, a bend. I waved my left hand around. Empty space. I was frightened of letting go of the pipework, losing contact with the guiding metalwork… my only connection to life.

I dropped to my knees. Concentrate. I crawled straight ahead for about ten feet. Then I reversed. When I found that I could feel the pipe work again I felt calmer about things, a little braver. I crawled again, a slightly different direction. My hand touched something, more metalwork. I felt it. It felt like… my hand explored more… it was a ladder! It was fixed to the wall. I pulled myself to my feet, feeling each rung. I still couldn't see anything.

Slowly, I climbed each rung. I went up eleven… then a door. I felt a door, a trap door. Hanging on, I used my free hand to explore… it felt as though, if I pushed here… it opened! It took all my strength, but it lifted up… and open. When I finally managed to crawl out I collapsed and cried with joy. I may have crawled into Hell as far as I knew, but anywhere was better than being where I'd just come from.

It was a big room, still dark, but in here I could make out shapes… machines… boxes… things. Dull light seeped through a window. As my eyes adjusted, I could see a door. I tried it… it wasn't locked! I peeped through the opening and made out a small car park and a garden area… It was the grounds of Wylander House!

I hadn't a clue what time it was, though it felt like the early hours of the morning. I needed to get away. Gilbert was bound to find me if I didn't. There was a pile of old cardboard boxes. I sat amongst them to plan my next move. Voices woke me. Bright sunlight streaked through the dirty window. Doors banged.

Day 13 Tuesday

I peeked through the window. Right alongside was a big black car. The back door closest to me was open, and sitting in the back were two girls. Across the other side of the yard, two Gilberts were pulling out the contents of a building. They were looking for something... or somebody!

I carefully opened the door, slipped out, crawled into the back of the car and lay down at the girls' feet. They didn't flinch! What's more, the one closest to the door pulled it shut. They must have figured out that it was me the Gilberts were searching for and for some reason decided to help me out. A silent few minutes later somebody climbed into the driver's seat and we were off.

We drove for ten minutes, and then pulled over. This was my lucky day. I prodded the girls' legs, to get their attention. I wanted them to open one of the back doors so I could slip out. I hoped they could figure out that that was what I wanted.

A door opened, but it wasn't opened by either of them.

"Hello there." He wasn't an old bloke. Smart, dressed in a dark suit. "Wouldn't you be more comfortable sitting on a seat?"

I slowly pushed myself up. "Thanks for the lift mate, hope you didn't mind."

"Not at all. Take a seat."

"It's alright, I can walk from here."

"Where to, back to Wylander House? I'll drive you back if you like."

"No, it's fine, just drop me here, thanks."

"Look son," he said as he held open the door, although it was obvious he wasn't intending to let me out.

I tried the other door, it wouldn't open.

"They don't open from the inside," he said, smugly. "Sit back and enjoy the fact that I'm not taking you back to Gilbert Welsh and his mates… not yet anyway." He slammed the door shut and returned to the driver's seat. "If you behave yourself," he said over his shoulder as the car fired into life, "you can join the girls and have the great pleasure of meeting Lord Filrothe."

Both girls eyed me up and down without speaking. I sat directly behind the driver. The girl immediately beside me was dark haired, about thirteen. In fact both of them were about thirteen years old. The other one was blond. Before old smarty pants the driver had mentioned that we were to meet Lord Filrothe, I'd assumed that we were off on the school run. Both girls wore school uniforms, checked light blue dresses and long white socks. When I said hello, both just about cracked a smile. Arrogant tarts. The driver either laughed or coughed.

I sat back and thought about my situation as the car sped along to wherever it was headed. Lately, my life was full of surprises. However, I couldn't bring myself to believe that sitting in the back of a big, plush comfortable car was a stroke of good luck. I know it was better than being lost in the hospital tunnels or being in the clutches of Gilbert and his cronies, but I also knew that meeting this Lord Filrothe wasn't going to be a good thing. This was the bloke I'd overheard the Tottenham Turk talking about; Lord Filth, paedo, associate of Charlie Farthin. I shivered at the thought, even though the car was nice and warm, and very comfortable. I was soon asleep.

Chapter 33

Smarty Pants woke me by tapping on the window of the car. His stupid grin wasn't the best sight after a deep sleep, quite scary. It took me a few moments to come round properly and remember where I was and what I was doing. The girls had gone.

Standing behind the grinning idiot was a much older bloke, rocking on his feet, hands behind his back. His shirt had dribble marks all down the front and his stomach was too big.

Smarty opened the door, recoiled and waved a hand, as though I stank. "I can't believe you thought you could hide in here, smelling like that. And I definitely can't believe I brought you here to meet his Lordship. It's some wonder that I still have a job. Come on, out."

I didn't move.

"Out!"

I was still half asleep, and slumped out of the car. Smarty grabbed the shoulder of my hoodie and yanked me upright.

"Take it easy James." The older bloke stepped forward. "This young man is a guest of Filrothe Hall. We can't have him pushed and pulled about like he was a naughty puppy, ha ha ha."

He was really posh, but I appreciated the concern. Smarty let go of my jacket and took a step back. "Yes sir."

"Now young man, let's have a look at you," and he walked around me. "You look as though you've had a torrid time, I wonder if you're hungry. Would you like something to eat?"

"Yes please Mister." I sounded like Oliver Twist.

"Do we have a name?"

We? What the fuck was the bloke on about?

Smarty jabbed me in the back. "Tell his Lordship your name."

"Oliver… Sir."

"Oliver." The Lordship grabbed my right hand and shook it. "Oliver. Well I'm very pleased to meet you Oliver. Come, stand by me, come and look at our little house." He placed a hand around my shoulder and we stood looking at a house as big as Saint Hels. "If you are a good boy and do as you are told, I'll show all the delights of Filrothe Hall, there are some wonderful places to play. James, take Oliver to Miss Stiggles, she can take care of the boy. You need to find the yard boys and give the Bentley a clean, you have people to collect this afternoon."

"Yes Sir."

"And tell Miss Stiggles that I would like Oliver to join us this evening."

"Certainly Sir."

The Lordship turned and marched off.

"Join him, what does he mean?"

"It means he wants you to join him this evening."

We didn't go through the big doors at the front of the building, which I'm sure would have been the quickest route. Smarty took me around the back. Miss Stiggles looked just like Mrs Andrews, the deputy head at Saint Hels... thin and tall... short, mousy, greasy, hair... glasses... but Miss Stiggles had a beard.

She was really stuffy, I think she was put out by my presence, and huffily led me up a flight of narrow stairs and along a corridor without saying a word, until... "Right Oliver," as we entered a bedroom. "Get undressed."

"What, no fuckin way!"

"Boy, you stink. Get those clothes off now and get into the shower before you contaminate the whole house."

"I ain't gonna take anything off in front of you!"

"Please yourself." She grabbed my hand and twisted it up my back.

"Owwweee..." It fucking hurt.

She undid my jeans and they fell around my ankles. I tried in vain to hold on to them, stop them falling, but the cow jerked on my arm, which hurt like hell. Then my pants!

"Right. Now you look really stupid. If I let go of your arm, will you undress?"

I felt stupid. "Yeah," nodding like mad.

She let go of my hand. "Take everything out of your pockets, throw your clothes on the floor, there," she pointed, "and get into the bathroom."

I did as she said, as fast as I could, and I didn't like the way she looked at me while I did so. Once completely naked, I scampered into the bathroom, glad *that* little episode was over. But, as usual with me, it wasn't.

I was just getting my bearings... shower... basin... when she marched right in. It was a small bathroom, way too small for two!

"Here is a tooth brush and paste." She opened the glass door of the shower cubicle. "Soap, shampoo," pointing. She liked to point. "Make sure that you clean every single part of your body... thoroughly. Understand?"

I nodded, embarrassed..

"Towels." More pointing. "I've sent for a sandwich, it will be ready and waiting by the time you've washed and dried." She turned on the shower. "Teeth first."

I grabbed one of the towels and wrapped it around myself... then cleaned my teeth. Or I thought I had.

"Clean them properly. Back ones as well... and use the mouth wash."

She was a real cow. The lid on the toilet was down, and she sat on it... the bitch was making herself comfortable, she was *only* going to watch me shower! How could I wash properly with her looking on? The only, slightly, saving grace was that everywhere was getting steamed up.

"Shower!"

By the time I'd finished I had washed every square millimetre about one hundred times. I was already tired and the warmth of the shower threatened to push me over the edge, I no longer cared that *she* watched, instructed, ordered. When I climbed out of the cubicle it took super human effort to stay upright, all I could think about was collapsing onto the bed and sleeping. Almost...

Two big, hot, bacon sarnies waited as I fell out of the bathroom, but I was so hungry I didn't even taste them before they had gone.

"Just a few questions..."

"Ohhhh please."

"Have you ever had sex?"

"What!"

"Tell me."

"I nodded.... yeah."

"With a girl?"

"Yeah."

"How many girls?"

Er, let me think.

"You need to tell me the truth, I'll know if you are lying."

"How?"

"I'm a trained nurse."

"What does that mean?"

"It means that I'll know if you are lying."

"One."

"Men?"

"Men!"

"Yes. Have you ever had sex with a man, or many men?"

How could I lie. "No."

"Good. Do you have any medical problems?"

I shook my head. "No, just tired."

"Now. I'm going to take your blood pressure, and some samples... blood, urine..."

Fuck. By the time she had finished with me I was more than exhausted... I didn't care why she wanted to know so much about me, and I don't remember her leaving. The next thing I knew, she was back with my clothes, cleaned and ironed. She said it was nine o'clock. I dragged myself from the bed.

She went to the bathroom and returned with a cold flannel and cleverly used it to wake me properly. It was a trick she'd learnt in a Japanese prison-of-war camp.

I dressed.

"Are you ready young man?" as I preened myself in the mirror.

I shrugged, ready for what? I picked up the hoodie.

"You don't need your jacket. Leave it here."

I collected all the stuff I'd removed from my pockets earlier, put it back into their proper places, then followed Miss Stiggles down some wide stairs and into a large kitchen. Noisy laughing and shouting came from another part of the house, which we ignored.

Sitting at a wooden table were the two girls who had travelled with me earlier. I'd forgotten all about them. "Hi," I said, also forgetting that they were a bit snooty.

They looked at me like I was bad news.

"Hello girls," said Miss Stiggles. She got the same response.

Anyway, I sat beside the dark one, Blondie sat opposite, and Miss Stiggles disappeared.

As soon as the three of us were alone the girls changed. "I'm Grace," whispered the dark one, "She's Hanna."

Grace gently stroked my hand. "Why are you here?"

"It's a long story. You?"

"Don't you know why?"

I realised I hadn't thought about it. "Since I've been here I've been asleep, or eating, or being scrubbed an' interrogated by that mad woman, so I haven't thought about it."

"Why did you get into the car, this morning?" asked Hanna.

I shrugged. "It seemed a good idea at the time. If I hadn't I'd probably be dead by now. So this must at least be better than that."

Miss Stiggles returned, and the girls went quiet again. Without speaking, she placed sausage and chips and buttered bread in front of the three of us. I was hungry enough to dive straight in and most of it had gone by the time salt and vinegar arrived at the table. Both girls played with their food, nibbling at it. As I scoffed, they topped up my plate. When the three plates were wiped clean I sat back and sighed. What I needed now was a drink. Just as though she had read my mind, the bearded lady replaced the three empty plates with three glasses of coke."

Yessss! I reached forward for one of them. Grace squeezed my leg under the table and sternly looked me in the face. What! I pulled my hand away, and we all sat, silently looking at the bubbly glasses. Miss Stiggles was busy pottering around at the sink and hadn't noticed Grace's weird behaviour, and eventually, when she disappeared from the room again, I had questions.

"What yer doing? I need a fuckin drink."

"It's drugged."

"What!"

"They're drugged, the drinks. She's gonna drink her's." Grace nodded towards Hanna. "But I'm not. You need to know what's going on before you decide." Grace's hand was back on top of the table, touching mine, and it was shaking.

I was silent, wondering what the hell they were on about.

Hanna leaned forward. "What's the matter with you?" She was speaking to me. "Are you really so thick, you don't know what's happening?"

"No." I shook my head.

"Fuck. I don't believe it."

"Leave him alone Han. It's not his fault if he don't know."

Hanna leaned forward even further, one eye on the door, I noticed. "We're tonight's entertainment. Them noisy fuckin perverts are gonna..." She fell silent as the door swung open.

"Drink up you three."

Hanna grabbed her coke and downed it. I really need a drink, but...

Grace swapped her full glass for Hanna's empty one, and Hanna gulped that down as well. Both looked at me. Was this a trick, to get my coke? Well, in case it was, mine slid down my throat without touching the sides. Aaaahhhh Heaven.

"Time to go to the party," sang out Miss Stiggles.

The next thing I remember, I was back in my room, naked and laying on top of the bed. My clothes were strewn across the floor. I was groggy as I lay, not wanting to move. It was daylight outside... the morning after...

Chapter 34

Day 14 Wednesday

I stayed on the bed and drifted back to sleep.

When I woke again I had a blanket on top of me, my clothing was in a neat pile on a chair and there was a plate of sandwiches, covered in cling film, on the bedside table. I tried to force myself into a sitting position… I hurt. My legs hurt, my groin. My cock ached. Then I realised that I hurt like I'd hurt after Michael Deer attacked me! Bastards!

I remember only as much as I've already told. I felt dirty all over, my skin didn't feel right. I went into the bathroom where I scrubbed myself thoroughly and cleaned my teeth, Miss Stiggles would have definitely approved. I dressed and sat on the bed. After a while I ate the sandwiches and wondered about the girls… about Grace, and decided to go and see them. The door was locked. Force didn't work. I checked the window, also locked. Anyway, it looked a long way down, too far to think about escaping that way. I still wasn't myself, and again dropped off to sleep.

The next time I woke, it was voices that woke me. Outside my room I could hear Lord Filrothe talking with a woman. She was asking him about the committee, how the meeting went. She didn't sound as though she'd been at the 'party' the night before…

"Help. Let me out. Unlock the door," I shouted.

Filrothe said something.

"Who's in there?" a woman's voice.

"I am. Let me out. I'm a prisoner!"

The door knob turned but the door didn't open.

The woman's voice again. "Open the door… where's the key?"

"Leave the door alone!" Filrothe. A struggle… then a wild shout. "JAMES!"

There was a smash against the door.

"Leave the door alone young lady!"

Another smash, and a crack. More struggling, and a heavy thud… one of them was down. I waited, breath held. Then another smash, a crack, and the door swung open, sending me flying. A woman stood where the closed door had been. Eyes scurrying around the room before settling on me. Behind her Filrothe had pulled himself upright.

"Look out!" I shouted as he lunged towards her.

She swung around and elbowed the older man right on the nose… blood spattered. "Come on," she beckoned.

I didn't need telling twice, and jumped up onto my feet and followed her towards the top of the stairs. "Wait!"

"What?" Annoyed

"GRACE… HANNA!" I shouted.

Voices. "In here, over here… the door's locked!"

"Fuck… how many of you are there?"

"Just the three," as we followed the shouting. Down a short corridor off the hallway.

The woman wasn't particularly big, but it only took two shoulder barges to break the lock. The girls weren't as stupid as me, and had stood clear as the door flew open. Then we went for it. Miss Stiggles was sent flying by our rescuer at the foot of the stairs and we made it into the yard. Hanna was almost carrying Grace, who looked in a really bad way. I took her other arm.

"Come on, my car is over there, the red one."

Behind us, Filrothe appeared at the large entrance. "STOP! JAMES!"

Smarty Pants had emerged from a building on the opposite side of the yard, two younger guys behind him. We were closer to the car than they were… but Grace was struggling. The lady made it easily and fired up the vehicle. Please don't leave us!

Smarty pants had us, bearing down really fast, aiming to intersect our path to the car.

"Leave me," cried Grace.

"Fucking got you…" Smarty just a few feet away… when a red block of hard metal smashed into him, then over him, as the lady reversed the car.

"IN!" She shouted.

We clambered in, closed the doors, the wheels spun and we shot forward in almost one instant movement. I looked back and saw the two other guys, Filrothe and Miss Stiggles rushing towards Smarty Pants, who was still spread out on the ground. We couldn't hear what was being shouted, but Filrothe was definitely shouting as he waved his fist in our direction.

We must have looked a poor sight, huddled up on the back seat, and the lady must have wanted to stop and find out what was going on, but she kept going, even when she'd reached the end of the long drive that led to Filrothe Hall. She sped on for quite a while, just asking if we were alright, until she turned down a side road. Then she pulled over.

"What has happened?" as she turned to look at us.

At first, none of us answered.

"Come on, I could be in a lot of trouble, helping you. You owe it to me to tell me."

"We were prisoners." I said.

"Yeah, okay. For how long?"

"Since yesterday."

Silence.

Grace took it up. "We were taken to the house yesterday, and last night they did things... Who are you?"

"My name is Reese Harrison, I'm a freelance journalist, and was visiting Lord Filrothe on behalf of a Sunday broadsheet, tying up a few loose ends to finalise a newspaper report. Money raised, progress made, latest news, etcetera, on 'Get U', a charity organisation that polices public and private institutions, to stop the mistreatment of vulnerable children. Lord Filrothe is Chairman of *Get U*."

We followed that with silence.

"I hadn't been invited, but wanted to be at the meeting, held yesterday afternoon. However, I was involved in an accident and couldn't make it. I turned up this morning, unexpected. Your turn."

Grace started to cry. "I hurt."

Reese climbed from the car and opened a rear door. "Hurt? Tell me. What has happened to you?"

Hanna pulled Grace into her, protecting her friend. "What d'yer think?"

"I think lots of things. But I'm a journalist, *you* need to tell *me*."

I'm not sure whether we were embarrassed or didn't trust the woman. But she had saved us, and was entitled to know. "Last night we were drugged..."

"I wasn't drugged, I'm Grace," butted in Grace. "This has happened before, lots of times, by others as

242

well. So this time I didn't let them drug me, so that I would be able to remember everything they did... an' names and faces. I want to go to the newspapers an' drop this lot in the shit."

I could see the woman becoming excited, it showed in her eyes. "I'm *the newspapers*. Tell me."

"Will I get money?" asked Grace.

"If this story is true and as big as I think it might be, you'll all be well looked after."

"We should go to the cops," I said.

The woman shook her head vigorously, "No, not yet. These people will pay for what they've done, don't worry."

"It's not that... Gilbert an' Charlie Farthin... they'll be after us."

I felt Grace take a deep breath.

Reese asked, "Who's Gilbert... and Charlie Farthin?"

I was surprised she didn't know, but then I hadn't known until a few days ago. "Gangsters. They're gonna be after us."

"We'll protect you, the newspaper will keep you safe, promise. Let's get to somewhere safe, so we can talk."

"It has to be somewhere where there are lots of people," said Hanna.

"It would be better at my flat."

Hanna obviously still didn't trust the woman, not completely, and I don't think she wanted to be taken somewhere that could still turn out to be another prison. "No. It has to be somewhere busy."

Reese shrugged. "Okay," and returned to the driver's seat. "How about a pub? We can sit in the garden, so that nobody can overhear our conversations."

This worried me. *A few people around* wouldn't stop Gilbert, especially not now that the cat was out of the bag regarding Lord Filrothe. "They killed my friend, shot him, an' they're after me cos I know too much. They want me dead, an' now they'll want Hanna an' Grace dead, an' I reckon they'll want you dead as well."

A hesitation. "Perhaps we should go to my flat." Reese was making some sense.

"No, a public place," demanded Hanna.

Grace had her eyes closed. "Maybe we should go to a hospital," I said.

Hanna stroked her friend's forehead and Grace's eyes flicked open. "I'll be alright."

The car moved forward and gathered speed. "There's a nice pub, a few miles from here. I'll phone my editor and he'll arrange for protection. We'll get a doctor for Grace."

I was still worried as we turned into a huge, and busy, pub car park.

Chapter 35

A wooden fence, like they have in America, in cowboy films, separated the car park from a lawn with loads of wooden tables on, each one having a big cream umbrella. Most tables had customers sitting at them, enjoying the sun. As luck had it, one group left their table as we arrived, and we replaced them. There was a joyful, noisy buzz about the place, which meant privacy for us.

Grace managed to make it to the table without attracting any attention. Reese had a large black leather bag, which she opened a soon as we'd sat down.

She pulled out some photographs. "All of you, look at these. Were any of the people in these photos at Filrothe Hall last night?" She handed them around. A girl collecting glasses collected the empty ones from our table, left by the previous people. "Can we order some drinks?" asked Reese.

"You have to go to the bar, madam."

"One of the girls is not well and I don't want to leave her, the others are too young to go to the bar."

The girl thought about this and, reluctantly, took the order.

"He was there," said Grace, pointing at the picture in front of her. And her."

"Yeah… I think I remembered her," I said, "It's blurry… but."

Reese was obviously excited. "That's Lindsey Digsdale, Lady Digsdale, Cabinet Minister. You *must* be certain."

"I'm certain," said Grace. "I remember her."

Reese's hands were shaking. "I think we should get out of here. I'll phone my editor." She pulled out her smart-phone, trawled through her contacts and waited for a reply… "He's not answering… Hi, Malc. Get back to me. This is very urgent," and hung up. She sent him a text as well.

She turned back to us. "These twelve photographs are pictures of the members of the charity, 'Get U'. Can you pick out any more who were at the… who were with you last night?"

I couldn't remember any, not definitely anyway, other than, of course, Lord Filrothe. Hanna was not much different, except, "This bloke," she fingered one of the photos."

However, Grace remembered all the others who were there. Four pictures were returned to Reese's bag. The rest stayed on the table, until the girl turned up with four cokes.

"What about *The Home*, where you sleep?" Reese asked me.

"I don't live at a Home. I live in Colchester."

"What about your parents?"

"Parents! Some parents. My dad sold my brother Josh into slavery, last week. I'm here now because I'm searching for him."

Reese nearly wet herself, she excitedly ruffled through her leather bag and pulled out a tape recorder. She switched it on. "Your father sold your younger brother into slavery. Why did he do that?"

"Because he owed Charlie Farthin money an' needed to pay him back."

This time she almost fell off her seat. She rubbed a hand across her head. "Where do I start? I can't believe this."

"It's true!" I said.

"Yes, I didn't mean that I don't believe you." She nibbled on her finger nails. "God!"

"Why was Gilbert after you?" asked Grace.

"Cos I'd found out too much. I was checking out Wylander House, asking questions. Then Gilbert took me to Friday Woods, to kill me, but my mate, Stick, saved me. The bastard got Stick though, shot him in the leg, then shot him in the head while he was on the ground." The image of Stick, on the ground, came back, clearly, and a tear formed.

247

Hanna, who was sitting next to me, kissed me on the side of the face and put an arm around me. "You have to get these bastards," she said to Reese. "If you double cross us, any of us, I'll get *you*!"

"I'm on your side."

"Wylander House is where me an' Hanna were at," said Grace.

"Had you been there long?" asked Reese.

"No. We came from Peterborough. We'd only been in Colchester for a few days."

"Peterborough?" Dek came from Peterborough. "Do yer know Dek?"

They both shook their heads.

"Had you been to see Lord Filrothe before you came to Colchester?" asked Reese.

"I've met him twice before," said Hanna.

"Three times," added Grace, "for me it's been three times."

"What about a girl called Dais... Daisy? Fifteen, straight blond hair, about my height. Did you see her at Wylander House?"

Hanna shrugged. "We never saw no-one. They kept us in a room."

Reese persisted. "Were the others, you know, Lindsey Digsdale, and the others from last night, were they at the previous get-togethers?"

Hanna didn't know. "We don't remember much about the other times… I don't remember much about last night. It's only Grace talking about what she remembers makes me remember things." She fidgeted. "How I hurt in places, that's how I mostly know about it."

Grace laid her head on her forearms, on the table. She really didn't look too good, it was obvious that she'd had a much worse time than me or Hanna. Her situation prompted Reese to try her editor again. I wanted to pee, and spied a sign pointing to the toilets. "Back in a minute."

You might find this hard to believe, but I'd never actually been in a pub before, and was fascinated by the hubbub of it all. Far better than, say, McDonald's. I could see the attraction. After I'd been to the loo I hung around the bar area, soaking up the atmosphere. It also gave me some thinking time.

I didn't know how long it had taken Smarty Pants to drive from Wylander House to Filrothe Hall, on account that I'd been asleep, but I thought it was probably a couple of hours. I needed to make sure, by asking the girls, or even Reese might know. The point was, I figured we probably had about an hour before Gilbert and his mates got to this area, and then they'd have to find us, so we had *some* time on our side. But, to do what? Grace needed to see a doctor, that was a priority.

If Reese was right about the people at the party being politicians and stuff like that, we were all in trouble. Okay, I was in trouble anyway, but now those three were in it up to their necks as well. I just needed to convince them of that fact. Reese seemed a bit of a know-it-all.

What would I do if I was Lord Filrothe? He's a big time paedo, and now he must assume that a journalist and three kids were about to expose him. He'd want us dead. Smarty Pants might be dead, after being run over by Reese, and Filrothe would have contacted Charlie Farthin… Charlie would have known straight away that the kid called Oliver was me.

The police were mixed up in it as well, I'd seen them at Wylander House, and they had looked well chummy with the Gilberts. We couldn't take a chance going to the cops, despite what I'd said earlier. No… Reese's newspaper was the best option, had to be. I had to tell her to drive us to her newspaper, she had to arrange medical help for Grace. An ambulance could meet us at where-ever the newspaper place was. Reese wasn't taking this serious enough… it was time for me to take charge. The bright sunlight blinded me as I returned to the garden.

Grace didn't look any better and Reese was busy asking Hanna about 'life in care'.

"Did you contact the editor?" I asked Reese as I sat, interrupting whatever she was asking Hanna.

"No. He's still not answered or got back, which *is* a little odd."

I smelt a rat. "I think we should leave here, go to your newspaper and arrange for an ambulance to meet us there, for Grace."

"We'll drink up and go."

I looked at the newspaper woman straight in the eye. "You don't understand. If Gilbert an' his gang find us, they'll kill us. Lord Filrothe probably sent for them ages ago."

"He's right," agreed Hanna, "we should get out of here."

Reese sighed, "Okay." And she began packing her leather bag with her interviewing gear. The glasses were empty anyway.

As I scanned the area my heart dropped through the floor. Standing at the entrance onto the lawn from the car park were two shaven headed thugs, looking directly at us. I turned to the entrance to the pub. Another one stood there. Shit. "It's too late."

Hanna and Reese first looked at me, then Reese followed Hanna's gaze, first the gate, and then the pub.

"Do you know them? Are you sure it's them?" asked Reese, desperation in her voice.

"No, never seen em before, but I know a Gilbert when I see one."

"That's fucking stupid," said Reese. "They could be anybody."

"Yeah, they could be," replied Hanna for me. "Why don't you try to leave?" Hanna knew, as well as I knew.

"Call the police," I urged her, "dial nine, nine, nine. But don't let them see you do it."

"What shall I tell them?" she asked.

"Tell em fuckin anything… tell em there's a dead body under the table…"

She fumbled with her phone.

As she did so, the glass collector picked up our empty glasses from the table, then placed a hand on top of Reese's hand. "Don't use the phone! I'm going to take it from you, if you make a fuss, you'll all be very sorry." She gently slipped her hand under Reese's, covering the mobile, removed it and placed it onto her tray, along with the glasses.

Reese stared, open mouthed, as the girl walked away with the mobile. "She can't do that!"

"She's just done it," said Hanna.

Grace stirred.

"How you feeling?" I asked.

"Crap." She was shivering.

"Can you walk?"

She shrugged. "Suppose so, why?"

"Gilbert's blokes are here."

She sighed.

"Where we walking to?" asked Hanna.

"Look. It looks as though there are three of em. There are four of us. If we all walk in different directions, one of us has to escape… whoever that is has to get to the police… not the newspapers… an' raise the alarm."

Hanna stared at me. "Is that the best you can come up with? We're fucked."

"It's our best chance," said Reese. I could see that she was getting ready to run… she was banking on her being the one to get away.

Hanna, open mouthed, shook her head in disbelief as Reese jumped to her feet, kicked off her high heels, and made a dash for it. Credit where it's due, she could move, and made a bee-line for the open field, the opposite direction from the car park and the pub. The three of us were flabbergasted as she hitched up her short skirt and clambered over the wooded fence, showing off her bum to the world. All the customers were staring, very interested in what was happening.

"So much for fuckin team work," I said.

Hanna laughed. Both baldies from the gate and the one from the pub took chase. "I bet they're gonna have a good time," she said.

"Who gives a fuck, let's get out of here," I said, jumping from the seat. I grabbed Reese's bag, we helped Grace to her feet and made our way towards the car park.

"What do we do now?" asked Hanna.

We sat down on a grassy space between a parked car and a hedge. I shrugged.

"Hanna." Grace moaned. She pulled a hand from between her legs, it was covered in blood.

"Oh God Grace!" Hanna turned to me. "She needs help, now. What can we do?"

In the distance a siren. "Listen. Somebody must have called for the police. We've no choice, we'll have to chance it an' trust em. Grace's gonna die if she don't get help."

"No!" cried Grace.

Hanna swore, "What d'ya have to say that for. You ain't gonna die Grace," hugging her.

I bit my lip. Two police cars turned up and their occupants jumped out and rushed onto the beer garden. Words and pointing, then two of the four policemen climbed over the fence and jogged off. One copper went back to his squad car and began talking into his radio.

"Go an' take Grace to him," I nodded towards the cop on the radio. "I reckon you'll be okay."

"You come as well," said Hanna, "It'll be safer than staying here."

"No. I need to find my brother. I won't be able to do that in a police cell."

"Will we be in a cell?"

"Not you, I don't think. But they think I killed Stick, an' also two other guys, gangsters."

Hanna just stared at me.

"Go," I said. Don't mention me until you're both safe, at the station. Then you can tell em everything you know about me. Tell em I ain't killed no-one."

"We don't know much about you to tell, but we'll tell em you ain't killed no one, def."

I rolled beneath a four by four and watched Hanna virtually carry Grace over to the police car. The cops didn't hang around, they didn't have to be doctors to realise that Grace was in a bad way, and one of the cars was soon on the move, siren blasting. I hoped the girls would be safe... I hoped we'd done the right thing. What choice had we had?

Chapter 36

The way the cops had reacted on seeing Grace made me wonder if I should give myself up as well. But how would that help Josh or Dais? On the other hand, if I ended up dead in a ditch somewhere or other, that wouldn't help them either. So that was my dilemma, come up with a really good plan, or hand myself in. I had a headache.

Police cars kept arriving, I lost count. It seemed as though nobody was leaving, I should think it was because the cops were questioning everybody. Two shoeless and dirty feet suddenly appeared beside my four-by-four. They moved back and forth and stood on tip toe as their owner checked out the activity going on in the beer garden. I didn't recognise them but I had a pretty good idea who they belonged to. I stuck my head out between the ankles. A bit pervie, but that wasn't my intention.

"Psssst…"

Reese looked around.

"Hey."

She looked down, snapped her thighs together, and became angry. "What are you doing?"

"It's me."

"I know it's you. Get out from under there and behave."

"I'm hiding. You need to get down here."

"No."

"I've got your bag."

She was down on her knees in an instant. "Come out from under there. You're acting too suspiciously."

"I'm hiding."

She grabbed my hood and pulled. I crawled out, and we both knelt on the grassy patch that I'd occupied earlier with Hanna and Grace.

"Where are the girls?"

"With the police. Grace was bleeding, from… you know."

"Shit. That wasn't how it was supposed to happen."

"She wasn't well. That's more important than your story."

"It wasn't just a story, it would have been my big break,"

"Well, it still could be. She'll be alright once she's in hospital, you can see her then."

"Yeah, sure, but it won't be as straight forward."

I wasn't sure how to continue. Reese was being really selfish. "How did you get away from the Gilberts?"

"Gilberts?"

"Yeah, the three blokes who chased you."

"The fat, beer swilling, cigarette smoking blokes you mean."

"Yeah, the ones who'll rip you apart if they catch you."

"Well, they didn't catch me." She opened the bag and pulled out her car keys. "I've got another mobile in the car, what do you think?"

"If the police stop us, I think we'll be okay, it's just that they'll want to interview us. They'll keep me, cos of Stick an' Deer, but you'll be able to go."

"Don't forget I've just run over Lord Filrothe's man."

I'd forgotten.

Reese continued. "If we can, we need to get out of here."

"Where are we?"

"Not far from Stevenage. If we can get away, we'll go to the newspaper's regional headquarters, in Cambridge. Then we can plan what to do next."

"Give me your keys. If I can get your other mobile we can slip away, an' when we're far enough, we'll call a cab."

Reese handed me the keys. "You sure you want to risk it," she asked. "The phone will be under the dash, on the right of the steering wheel."

I rolled back under the four-by-four. Reese's red car was away from the edge, but not too close to the parked police cars and the bunch of cops. I checked everywhere, including the upper windows of the pub, which overlooked the car park. When I thought I was safe, I dashed, head down, across the clearing and bopped down beside her car. I looked at the fob in my hand, and pressed the bit that unlocked it. *Clunk.* I waited, but there was no reaction. I was about to open the door when I heard a familiar voice.

"Get in." It was Gilbert's.

I peeped through the windows of Reese's car. He was standing with his back to me, on the other side, holding open the back door of an old, big, grey motor... and he had a gun in his hand. Climbing in was Reese. As she sat beside another gorilla, she caught my eye.

She looked petrified.

"I don't want any trouble, understand?" Gilbert's rough voice demanded.

She nodded, fearfully.

Gilbert then walked over to the group of policemen. *Make a noise*, I mouthed to Reese. I hoped she understood what I wanted. The car had been reversed into the gap, ready for a quick get-away I suppose, which suited me. The boot clicked as I unlocked it. At the same time, Reese swore, and bent forward.

"What are you up too, tart?" and the gorilla yanked her back up.

"Fuck off," she wriggled and tried to elbow him. The car rocked as the brute got her under control.

All this was enough to give me the time I needed to open the boot, climb in, and gently close it again, unnoticed. There was other stuff in there, but still enough room for me. A little while later, two doors opened and people got in. One was Gilbert.

"Sorted. Let's get out of here."

"What about the boy?"

"Bert and Mickey are still here, with a bit of luck, they'll get the little bleeder. We need to get out of here, now…" the engine fired up and we were on the move.

It was a bumpy journey, and it was dark, but I managed to get reasonably comfortable. I had no idea of the direction we were travelling, which didn't matter because I had no idea where we'd started from. They talked, in the car, all the time we were moving, but I couldn't make out what was being said because of the engine and road noise. It was a pity I hadn't had the time to get Reese's mobile. I wondered if it had been a stupid move, sneaking into the car and hiding, which was becoming a really bad habit. At least I didn't smell like I had the day before. We travelled for a long time.

The worst was the last couple of minutes, it was a really bumpy ride and I really thought I was going to puke… but I made it… the car came to a halt and the engine was turned off.

They all climbed out of the car and it wasn't long before I was on my own. I waited for a few moments, and listened. I couldn't hear anything… I had to take a chance. Fingers crossed, I felt for a handle or a knob... there wasn't one! I was locked in! I tried to force the seats forward but they didn't budge.

What the fuck was I going to do? What I couldn't do was panic. But knowing I was trapped had me wanting to shout for help… I might suffocate! I could phone for help… the police. Where was my mobile? I told myself to relax, calm down... and think. If I kicked the boot lid hard enough, perhaps it would open. My mind was going in so many directions that I didn't get round to doing anything that stupid… a door opened and somebody climbed into the car…

The front passenger, I thought, the way the car dipped. Then, for a while, there was nothing… just the steady breathing and occasional deep cough of a lone male.

Then someone joined him in the front. "Right Mal," said a gravelly voice.

"Red?"

"A little chat." Silence, then, "We need to talk about Deer. You weren't happy about his demise."

"I don't like anybody getting shot."

"Deer was takin chances, gettin greedy. See, we got ourselves a nice little enterprise. We save unfortunate kids from a shit life on the street, nothin wrong with that, an' then pass them on to good homes or places of employment... an' make ourselves a few bob in the process. It's a nice, safe little business, almost legal. Every once in a while a kid turns up who ain't got no connections, nobody who cares about em, looking for em, get my drift. We pass one or two of those onto the Russian, for a few bob more. The trouble was, Deer wanted to pass too many to the Russian."

"What's wrong with that? His money's good."

"You know what the Russian wants em for?"

I visualised a shrug.

"Medical research, spare parts for rich oligarchs... or sex slaves for African Generals. Get the idea? There ain't nothin more appealing to the world's heathen rich than a nice piece of white European ass... ass that they can do with just as they please." Another bout of silence. "Now, I agree the money is good, an' if we've got a kid that ain't ever gonna be missed... then, okay, we'll sell. But Deer's been collecting just about anything that moves. Well I don't like it, an' the Russian, he ain't stupid, he don't like it either. So, he's agreed to take this shipment, on the condition that Deer an' his boys are taken care of."

"His boys?"

"Yes, his boys. Blake... an' you."

"I ain't one of Deer's boys."

"Well he recruited yer."

"But…"

"Not only that, Mal… or whatever yer fuckin name is… he's recruited a fuckin copper."

Silence.

"A fuckin copper. Code name Bonzo. Who the fuck came up with that… Bonzo Dog Doo Dah Band! Well, you're in right doggy doo dahs now."

The car lurched, as though there was a short struggle.

"Don't bother trying anything," said the one doing all the talking… Red. "I'm not gonna pop yer… no. I'm gonna pass yer on to the Russian… yer fit, young… ish… good looking. I'm sure he'll find somethin for yer," a laugh.

"I'm not a cop, Red… you've got me wrong… you're makin a mistake."

"Operation Bonzo… Metropolitan Police… D-e-t-e-c-t-i-v-e I-n-s-p-e-c-t-o-r Littleton! Serious Crime Squad. Get my drift? Now get out an' fetch yer gear."

They both got out. Then there was a click and the boot flew open and a Gilbert was looking straight at me. I thought I'd had it. He paused… then leaned in and grabbed the two bags, like I wasn't there. Before he closed the lid again he discretely slid a mobile phone onto the boot floor. "I can't believe my last day of fucking freedom is a duck farm in East Willock." He didn't close the lid enough for the catch to engage. For a change I had my wits about me and made sure it didn't open again when he let it go. Then they were gone.

I knew I should have used the mobile before doing anything else, but I didn't want to be stuck in the car and on my way back to Colchester... or Stevenage. East Willock. That was for my benefit... which was pretty damn quick thinking, considering his name was Bonzo. I carefully repositioned myself so I could see beneath the lid. There wasn't anybody in sight to the rear of the car, so I took a chance and carefully slipped out. So far, so good. There were two guys beyond the front of the car, quite a distance away... they had guns slung over their shoulders, machine guns. Christ!

I lay under the car and looked the place over. It was like a town square, or a wide street, a dead-end one, with big black wooden huts along the sides... I could see eight... ten! Plus there was a smaller brown one at one end, gates at the other... the entrance. There was one of the black ones just a few feet to the right, and it had a double doorway, like an old-fashioned garage door, which stood back from the edge of the front of the building. There was a three-foot covered area to hide in, like an alcove. If I could make it there, that would be a good start.

I waited until the two heavies were looking the other way and that the rest of the yard was clear before crawling across the small gap. Situated in the alcove I could now hear ducks... it sounded as though there were hundreds of them. I needed to make the phone call, but the ducks! I wanted to see them. The continuous quacking sounded as though there was more ducks in this building than I'd ever seen before, in my whole lifetime.

The doors weren't locked… I pushed one open until there was enough of a gap to squeeze through. Inside, the quacking was louder, although I still couldn't see the ducks. Another ten or fifteen feet further on there was another set of double doors, same as the ones I just came through. I pushed one open… It was the most brilliant thing. A mass of white ducks, thousands, it looked like a sea of white. And the noise! And the smell!

The building was massive, nearly half the size of a football pitch, and the ducks were really funny, waddling and quacking about. I wished Josh could see them.

Chapter 37

Just as I decided to go back outside and phone the police the door behind me started to move. Thinking quickly, I moved aside and stood against the wall… the door was pushed all the way open, trapping me behind it, and somebody stepped in… I pictured a baldie with a gun. He stood and looked at the sea of ducks for ages but, fortunately, didn't look behind the door. Then, when he decided he'd seen enough, he stepped back and closed me in again.

It was hot and the smell almost choked me. I wasn't too keen about phoning the police, Mo would be better. I checked the phone… no signal. I crawled out amongst the birds until I was right in the centre of the floor, where there was enough of one to make the call. Trouble was, when I did, I couldn't hear anybody, the damn noisy ducks! Then I lost the signal.

I had no choice… I called the emergency services. I could make out there was somebody there, just. What could I say? I told him/her who I was, and that I was the one who the police wanted to talk to about the killing of Michael Deer. "I'm at a duck farm in East Willock… there are men here with guns… machine guns… they've found out that Bonzo is a policeman… they're handing him over to the Russian… get here as fast as you can..." Then the door opened again.

I was already flat on the deck, but I rolled over to the edge of the building and got flatter. I covered myself with as much straw as I could. I could see them, three of them, all Gilberts, and they began to slowly wade through the ducks, kicking out if the birds didn't move fast enough.

They weren't the only danger though. Just a foot ahead of my face appeared the biggest spider I'd ever seen. Not just the biggest, but the nastiest and hairiest, with big fangs. It really freaked me out and I wanted to jump up and escape from it. I could sense it getting ready… ready to pounce and sink its fangs. A choice: spider or Gilberts. But I was saved… a duck ate it! Saved by a magnificent white duck! You can't believe how relieved I was, I could have kissed that duck!

Back to the Gilberts. The ducks piled on top of each other and on top of me getting out of their way. The baldies walked right past me and continued to the other end of the floor, where they conferred and then left by a small door near the corner. I checked the phone. It was still on, so I whispered *loudly*… "They nearly got me, get here quickly."

I turned it off. I didn't want it ringing and giving me away. I was becoming a pro! I needn't have worried though because loads of fans started up and the noise was awesome. After a few minutes the place began to cool down. I slid on my belly, using my elbows and knees to push myself along, all the time ready to stop and cover myself with straw again, until I reached the door that the three had left by. I tried to listen, but it was impossible. You will need to have heard a thousand ducks quacking and about twenty big fans whirring to understand what I meant. I had no choice but to chance it... to lift the catch and try to see if it was clear on the other side. Again, luck was on my side, and I slipped outside.

A concrete path went to the right and around to the back, but there was a gap between the big black wooden buildings, all overgrown with tall weeds. I slipped amongst them and crawled to the front so I could see the main yard; perfect place for me to hide and to observe. I watched for over half an hour. Gun toting Gilberts patrolled between the buildings and around the perimeter, checking the horizon all the time.

A black expensive car, a short fat limo, ambled its way along the lane, pulled up in the yard, and four blokes climbed out. Two had guns. A little while after that, a lorry arrived.

There was a lot of hand shaking. The lorry driver, four from the limo and five Gilberts all stood around, some talking, most not. One of the four from the limo wore a smart suit, the sort of thing the prime minister wears; jacket and tie, even though the sun was shining and it was warm. He seemed to be talking mostly to a Gilbert with a red face... I wondered if that was *Red*.

A controlled shout... a quick command, and all bar a couple of Gilberts disappeared inside... and a police car turned up. Saved! Two cops got out and greeted the two Gilberts, shook their hands. Strangely though, the Gilberts continued to flash their guns.

The red faced Gilbert waltzed out and greeted the cops. I wish I could have heard what was said, because the cops pointed towards the big black buildings, speaking at the same time, and then it looked as though Red *thanked* them, shaking their hands and patting their backs. Then the cops wrote some stuff down, spoke on their radio, and left.

None of this made sense. Unless you were a squaddie or a cop you couldn't carry guns, not in England. And yet these cops hadn't said anything… they were bent! Had to be! The cops were in on it as well, whatever *it* was? I had the phone and needed to get in touch with the gang, get them to talk to everybody and anybody… then something hard touched the back of my head… the nozzle of a machine gun.

A Gilbert! Smiling. His teeth all crooked and brown. "Red… I've found im," he shouted, and he shoved me out into the open, prodding me with the barrel of his gun.

Immediately three more stood around me, including Red. "This is getting better and better," he said, "the goods are deliverin themselves, that's what I call efficiency." He dribbled as he laughed.

I was pushed hard and stumbled over, grazing my knees.

"Hey, careful, the Russian won't accept damaged goods."

After they searched me and took the mobile, I was shoved through the doors of one of the buildings, into a big dirty room. A whole section of wall opened and I was taken through it and down a flight of stairs, into a big underground area with about six different doors. Through one was a corridor with rooms on either side. I was taken to one of them and thrown in. Already in there was the Gilbert cop.

"Hi son," he said. "Bad luck." He seemed depressed. "Did you manage to make a call… the mobile?"

I nodded, and then told him about the police turning up and giving me away, which made him really angry… "Bastards. We're in trouble now, boy. What the hell have you been playing at? What were you doing in the car? And in the service tunnel at the old hospital, that was you, wasn't it?"

Then I realised, this was the Tottenham Turk. I was disappointed that he was just a cop. "Trying to find my brother," and I told him about Josh and Dais going missing."

"Describe them."

I did.

"Your brother isn't here, but the girl is!"

My heart leapt. "Is she alright?"

"She's not hurt, but no, she's not alright, none of us are. Look kid, you seem to have done better than us, the police, in your little investigation, but don't you realise just what danger you've got yourself into?"

I told him everything, from the beginning. I told him about Deer, the rape (but not about my hard-on), the dogs, Stick, Dais and Emma, the Gilberts, my dad, Charlie Farthin…Lord Filrothe, Hanna and Grace… and Reese. He knew about Reese. I also told him that the police are after me.

During my tale he butted in or made a comment now and then, but mostly he listened. "Christ, you've really been through it. If we get out of this I'll make sure you're okay."

"Don't tell anybody about Michael Deer, what he did to me." I must have been mad to mention him, but I was frightened and I couldn't help myself.

"You have my word. But that's about the least of your problems at the moment. If you get out of this, ask to see Detective Superintendent Littleton… refuse to speak with anybody else, get that?"

I nodded.

"Tell him everything, everything. You can trust him."

"Are you an undercover cop?" I asked him.

"Yeah."

"One of the kids at school has an uncle who is a traffic warden an' because of this he keeps being beaten up."

"So?"

I shrugged, "Just sayin. What's it like?"

"How do you mean?"

"Having relatives beat up all the time because you're a cop."

He didn't reply. Perhaps he didn't have any relatives.

"I mean, you didn't have to be a cop, nobody forced you. I know a bloke who's the horny red devil… an' then there's Old Bob at the U's, he's the grounds man. There are loads of different things you could do other than becoming a cop."

"Where is this conversation going?"

I shrugged. "Thinkin aloud. It's just that I've got to work when I leave school an' I was wondering why I would want to become a cop."

"There's a lot of satisfaction in being a policeman, you know, arresting scum like that lot upstairs."

"Yeah, I can see that. Can I watch when you do it? When are you gonna do it?" I waited for a moment, and then added, "Are you glad you're a policeman now?"

"Right at this moment in time, I suppose I wish I'd chosen a different career." There was no furniture in the room and we sat against the walls, facing each other. "But, if we nail them, then I'll be glad I became a policeman. If the only thing I did in my life was to bring down this Russian, it'd be worth it."

"And what is it about, all this, and the Russian?"

"The Russian is a man called Ivan Ulonavic, used to be a Captain in the Russian army, fought in Afghanistan. He's also involved with the Russian Mafia in Moscow. He's the man responsible for collecting people from the United Kingdom. He buys them from gangs like the one here in Colchester, run by Charlie Farthing and Red Walton. His little set-up and the gangs, he collectively calls 'the association'. The gangs obviously know about him, but they don't know about each other. What we haven't found out, and want to… are there any more Ivan Ulonavic's, or who it is who actually carries out the shipping. We also have an idea that organised groups are grooming youngsters, vulnerable youngsters, for sexual pleasure or worse. I'm here trying to find answers to all those questions."

He went on. "People are exported and sold into the slave trade, all over the world. Usually it's into prostitution. Sometimes… worse. They could be sold for replacement parts, to the illegal medical industry. To supply hearts, lungs, livers, kidneys, eyes…"

"Eyes!" It was gruesome. I wondered what it would be like, my eyes… seeing in someone else's head?

He got really serious and crawled over, closer.

"What I think is going to happen now is, Ulonavic will decide who he wants to sell on. Anybody who he

273

doesn't want… will be murdered. I'm pretty certain I won't be wanted."

"What, they'll kill *you*? But you're a cop!"

"Don't be naïve kid. You saw how they killed your friend Stick. And you know what they did to Michael Deer and Pete Blake."

"Pete the sleaze."

"Well, I'm done for. But you're not. There's a good chance you'll be taken off somewhere. At the first opportunity, run. Go to the authorities, or if you're abroad, go to the police and demand to see somebody from the British Embassy, or any Embassy."

"Maybe they won't kill you… they might want to use you for spare parts. That'll give you some time, to escape."

He looked at me… had I said the wrong thing? And he hugged me, tightly, too tightly. "Good luck kid." And he wouldn't let me go for ages. I think he was crying. I couldn't wait to see Dais. She was here, that was the best news ever.

Chapter 38

"That's Red Walton."

We were sitting on the floor listening to the sound of voices coming through the walls, from all around.

"They're ducks."

He looked at me in despair. He'd already explained how we needed to look for any opportunity to escape because if we didn't we'd probably die. I figured that if we were going to die, why spend our last hours being so fucking serious. Funny thing though, it didn't matter how much he told me about our imminent deaths, all I could think about was Dais. I tried to listen out for *her* voice.

"Crap in the corner, in that bucket."

"What!"

"You heard. I won't look, if you're embarrassed."

"I ain't embarrassed, I don't want to go."

"Look kid, just do as I say. We're in for some hairy moments. I can promise you now, you'll feel better for it. And when it matters, you won't have your mind on the fact that you've crapped yourself."

That's the sort of conversation we had while locked up in that little room. I think he thought he was teaching me the art of survival but I don't think I was any better as his student than anyone else's. Anyway, fuck him. I didn't crap. The only thing he spoke about that was remotely interesting was on the subject of the machine guns; Uzis. He told me how to handle and load one, in case I got the opportunity.

I'd been estimating times, you know, what time did we leave Filrothe, how long at the pub, how long in the boot of the car… and how long me and the undercover cop were stuck in the room. Since dumping Stick's mobile, that's what I'd had to do; estimate. And because the cop wouldn't shut up I really couldn't tell how long we were together… an hour, ten hours? It could have been a month! Eventually a Gilbert opened the door. I was almost relieved.

He hauled both of us out of our *cell* and lined us up against the wall in the big underground room, just the two of us to start with. Then another bloke joined us, then more, until there were twelve, all men… or boys. Still no Dais though. The excitement was almost unbearable… waiting to see her! After about twenty minutes I began to think she wasn't here, that the undercover cop had lied for some reason. Then two girls were led out and placed alongside us. After that, another group; five. Hanna! What was she doing here? And Reese… I was genuinely glad that they hadn't hurt her. She looked so frightened though. Perhaps the fact that she was a journalist meant she had seen things, like the cop had seen things. Reese and the cop looked the most scared out of all of us.

Red entered the room. I could see why they called Red, Red. His face and his hair were red. No wonder he killed people. Then three more joined; three girls. Last out was Dais. She was beautiful!

I saw her face light up when she saw me… then she was sad again. I smiled. I wanted to go over and hug her, so glad she was okay. My whole insides were jingling.

The Russian strolled out, the one in the prime minister's suit, all smart, like a film star. He had a white silk handkerchief stuffed in his top pocket. Prat. He paced up and down the room, checking us out. One of the girls sniffled, but stopped as soon as he glared at her.

He halted, and faced us. "Who do you think is the most valuable one amongst you, to me?" he asked, placing his right hand on his left tit as he said '*me*'.

I didn't really know what he meant. There was silence all round.

"Answer me!" and he grabbed a bloke by the chin, squeezing his face. "Which one of you do you think is most valuable to me?"

The bloke jerked his head back in defiance, and the Russian released his grip. "I dunno… her," and he pointed at Dais.

She was easily the best looking girl. I suppose if he sold us, she'd easily fetch the highest price. He would if

I was buying, anyway. I smiled at that thought. The bloke was right, Dais was easily the best… I was actually quite proud.

The Russian walked over to Dais. "He is right," and he pulled her from the row and turned her to face us. "He is absolutely right. This woman is a work of art," he stroked the side of her head as he stood, half behind and half beside her. "She is a beautiful creature, one worth a great deal, in any money. This is the one I would have chosen also. Now though…" he paused and took a long look at us all, "I would like to give you a demonstration as to how important it is for all of you to follow orders. A demonstration to show you that, however valuable you may think you are, if you step out of line…"

I wasn't listening. I was well pleased. Dais, the most beautiful girl in the room. The Russian had taste, but I suppose anybody would have chosen her out of us lot. She was looking at me, and she was trembling, and I wanted to rush over to her, to tell her that we were going to escape; her, me and the undercover cop… and Hanna and Reese. A tear welled, broke and ran down over her smooth cheek… it was too much. I shouted her name and lurched towards her. No fucker was going to keep me from being with her. The undercover cop grabbed me by the arm as all eyes turned to me.

"This is what I mean," bellowed the Russian. "A demonstration to all of you who attempt to undermine me," and he pulled out a pistol and raised it to Dais' head.

"NO!" I screamed and lurched forward again. I think the undercover cop helped me on my way, because I seemed to be catapulted towards the smarmy bastard so fast that that I hit him as he pulled the trigger.

There was a loud crack and Dais jerked forward... disappearing from my view. In an instant Dais' head was replaced by a hand holding a gun. I collapsed on top of her... I wanted to protect her. I rolled her over a couple of times until we reached the edge of the room. She groaned... moved... and held her hand to her head... not much blood.

"You're alright!" I shouted. Now, all around, was mayhem. Suddenly a loud ratatat as a machine gun went off. Screams. The Russian was standing in front of where me and Dais lay, he was aiming his hand gun at the cop and was about to shoot. The cop was struggling with a Gilbert, trying to prise an Uzi away from him. I kicked the back of the Russian's leg, which messed up his aim, and two of the blokes who had been standing against the wall rushed forward and started to grapple with him.

Another Gilbert waded in and fought off the two and, along with the Russian, retreated from the room. Red was kicking out and threatening to have everybody shot but that didn't stop anybody. The cop now had an Uzi. One of the guys had one as well... there was a Gilbert face down on the floor. I hadn't seen him go down. Unarmed, Red backed away and made it to the exit door. The enemy had legged it.

That's when the undercover cop took control.

Me and him edged through the door and crept up the stairs to face Red Walton and the Russian and their thugs.

I came around, alone, in a ditch. I was lying down in the stream that trickled along the bottom, soaking wet, my heart thumping, and I was crying, not just crying... sobbing.

For a long time I didn't know anything, why I was crying, where I was, where I'd been. I couldn't even see anything other than the brightness of the sun. Then I blacked out, I think. I must have, because when I awoke again it was getting dark.

I was calmer. I pulled myself up the bank. Every part of me ached. I wasn't far from the duck farm.... it was eerily quiet. Dais' face flashed in my mind. I had to get back to the basement.

I staggered to my feet and made my way back towards the black buildings. I felt my body for bullet holes. The guns were Uzis, that's what the undercover cop had told me while we were in our little room. As I got closer I saw that the Russians' lorry was still there. But I couldn't see any Russians.

As I approached, the sound of quacking grew louder. I saw the door, the one where the cop and me had last been together. I slowly pushed it open and entered the gloomy room. It led to the basement, the lights were back on, and I listened for voices, but all I could hear were ducks. The big room at the foot of the stairs had been piled high with bodies. My hand trembled violently as I slowly went down…

When I reached the bottom, I stood. I didn't want to touch them… so I looked. There were two Russians and seven Gilberts, including Red, and the cop… the undercover cop! All dead!

There were others. Reese… she was still shoe-less. Hanna. Piled like sacks against a wall. And Dais. I pulled her away from the others, but she wasn't like Dais anymore… I dragged the cop across the floor, to lay next to her. I don't know why I did that, except I thought he deserved to have a special position. I stood over them and removed the St Christopher from around my neck and placed it on her chest. Using the tip of my finger, I placed a teardrop on the necklace.

"Take it with you."

I looked around. There was no one else in the room… not living. As I examined the bodies, looking for life, I began to tremble. A chill moved through my body.

"Take the necklace with you."

It wasn't Dais' voice, or anybody else I knew. In fact, it wasn't a voice… or it was… I can't explain. I picked up the necklace and kissed it. Was it you? I studied Dais' face, then slipped it over my head. "I love you," I whispered.

Four or five Uzis lay on top of the bodies and magazines were scattered about. Some were heavier than others and I collected three of the heaviest, the ones with more bullets. I took two guns and slung them over my shoulder.

I checked the huts, leaving the doors open as I did so, and soon the yard was full of thousands of ducks. Quack quack. Thank you. That's alright, it was the least I could do.

I found two more bodies; Gilberts. One was shot in the head. I went back and looked at the bodies in the big room. Most of the kidnapped had wounds all over their bodies but two of the Gilberts were like the other one; executed! Again I looked at Dais. Somebody, at least, had survived and finished off Red's men. The Russian wasn't amongst the dead. That was the moment I decided that him, Gilbert and Charlie Farthin had to be executed… and me? I had to be the executioner! That was my destiny. I hunted through the bodies for phones but didn't find any.

The ducks had started to disappear into the darkness. I covered my face in duck shit, rubbed it in, and, armed and dangerous, started to make my own way into the darkness, along the only lane that led from the farm.

Chapter 39

I should have hunted for food… they must have had food at the farm, and drink. Rambo would have looked… I needed to be more thorough. And I was cold. I walked and walked and walked. I'd never been in the country before, other than school outings, and that was years ago. They'd stopped taking kids like me on school outings a long time ago.

I kept telling myself that being in the country was just like being in the park, only the country was bigger. But it wasn't the same. For a start, they didn't have owls in the park. Fucking owls. I came across a big barn, half full of straw, and that saved my life. I had lost the garlic just when I probably needed it most, I was completely exposed to the elements. However, I snuggled down and got warm… the next thing I knew, it was morning.

Day 15 Thursday

It was as though I was born to do this. When I woke I knew exactly where I was and what I was doing… and what I was going to do… I was in a barn and I was going to hunt down Gilbert and Charlie Farthin. I wanted the Russian as well, badly, but I couldn't go to Russia... even I'm not that stupid! What I'm saying was... I was totally alert.

I checked everything and also practised changing a magazine on one of the Uzis. Then I stepped out into the open... and couldn't remember which direction I'd come from. Shit! The countryside was big enough as it was, without having to walk it twice. I sat on the verge, trying to figure it out, when I heard a car.

I could see it coming, really slowly, from miles away, and had plenty of time to decide what I was going to do. And what I was going to do was... I was going to highjack it. As long as there was only one person in it, even if it was a big bloke, I had the Uzi! I ignored the thought that he might have an Uzi as well... that was fucking stupid.

I stood back amongst some trees as it approached. I began to get nervous. There was just a driver. I jumped out and stood in the middle of the lane, one of the Uzis at the ready, and the car, a little green mini with a white roof, you know, the older type, pulled up.

I walked over to the window and an old lady wound it down. "Hello dear, can I help you?"

"Where are you going?" I pointed the gun in the window.

"Saxmundham dear, to visit my friend, Mrs Davies."

"Take me to Colchester," I demanded, waving the nozzle of the gun in her face.

"Are you taking me hostage?"

"Yeah."

"Ooh how exiting! I've never been a hostage before."

Well, that was fucking easy, and I climbed into the car beside her.

"Are you a scout?" she asked as we drove off.

"No."

"My great grandson is a cub, but he'll be scout when he's as big as you. Or is it the Boy's Brigade?"

"Is what the Boy's Brigade?"

"What you're in. Although I thought the boys in the Boy's Brigade wore uniforms. But I suppose if you are out on manoeuvres…"

"I'm not in the Boy's Brigade either."

"Oh." And she was quiet for a bit.

I think she was driving slower than I could walk, and I told her so.

"It's the ruts. If I drive too fast they'll break the suspension. Do you have to be in Colchester very quickly, because if you do, I'll phone my daughter. She's a faster driver than me, I'm sure…"

"No, it's okay. Just drive."

Eventually Mrs Dexter reached the main road. Mrs Dexter, that's what she told me her name was. She had four children, all girls, and they had nine children between them, who were all married, and three of them had children as well…

I was trying to work out a plan, and her father had just returned from the Great War; Mrs Dexter wasn't even born. Fuck. Then I thought of the phone. "You got a mobile?"

I had halted her in mid-sentence. "Pardon dear."

"Have you got a mobile phone?" I found myself raising my voice, I don't know why.

"Yes, of course. Samantha, that's my eldest grand-daughter, gave it to me, in case I was ever attacked, or taken hostage."

"Can I borrow it?"

"Of course you can dear, as long as using it is not cheating."

"Cheating?"

She nodded. "Good. I don't like cheating. It's in the glove compartment."

I phoned Fallon.

"*Hello.*"

"Fallon, it's me."

"*Fuck. Where are you?*"

"Where are we?" I asked Mrs Dexter.

"I'm not saying!"

There must have been other people I could have taken hostage. "I don't know… on my way back to

Colchester. Look, Fallon, tell Mo an' the others… I'm coming for Charlie Farthin."

"*What do you mean?*"

"They've killed Dais… an' the undercover cop… an' all the others. I'm gonna get Farthin… and Gilbert, an' the Russian if I can find out where he is. See if you can find out where he is."

"*Fuckin hell… you're mad.*"

"I'm not mad… I'm the Gay Avenger."

She hung up.

"Is that your code name dear… the Gay Avenger. But that's not a good idea, you know, these days a gay person is not a happy person. You should change your name to the Happy Avenger."

I was numb. Mrs Dexter resumed telling me the history of her family as we joined a bigger road. I told her to stop at a small store by the side of the road. "Wait here." I took off the Uzis and placed them on the back seat, under my jacket, "do you want anything?"

"I eat very regularly dear, at my age you have to."

I figured she meant no. Apart from the woman behind the counter the shop was empty and it didn't take long to get a couple of bottles of coke and biscuits and chocolate. I know what she said, but I bought a giant box of chocolates for Mrs Dexter. I noticed the assistant stand back as I approached her. I think I smelt.

"Do I smell?" I asked Mrs Dexter when we were back underway.

"Well… I was going to mention it… like a dirty duck."

As we passed Ipswich, Mrs Dexter gave birth to her first daughter, not long after Mr Dexter had returned from Berlin at the end of the Second World War. I asked her if we could listen to the radio.

"Not that awful music."

"What music is that?"

"The music you listen to. What about classical music?"

"What's that?" and she selected it. I listened and then we compromised by tuning in to Radio Colchester. We both agreed that the stuff they played was rubbish. As we hit the last leg, the A12 from Ipswich to Colchester, there was a news bulletin. Many murdered bodies ·had been discovered by police at a duck farm near Peasenhall, in Suffolk.

The old lady was silent as the story unfolded. '…thousands of ducks are running free across nearby farmland as hundreds of police descend upon the area in cars, vans and helicopters. Police are not denying that a number of bodies have been discoverd, dead from gunshot wounds. A huge police cordon is being set up as we speak…'

"Is that you?" She spoke very quietly.

"I was there when they were killed, I escaped."

288

"How?"

"I'm not sure… one minute I was fighting alongside the undercover cop, the next thing I knew, I woke up in a ditch."

Again she was quiet.

'…news has reached us that the killings were carried out by *The Gay Avenger*, and it's been reported that he's now on his way back towards Colchester to continue his killing spree…'

"It wasn't me… I'm not the killer… it's not fair!"

Mrs Dexter gently laid her hand on my knee. "Are you going to kill me?" Her question was as gentle as her touch and I started to cry.

'…residents have been advised to stay inside and lock their doors and windows and it has been reported that incidents of road rage are occurring as cars flee the town… Police urge people to stay calm and that there is no way that the Gay Avenger will be able to gain entry into the town… even if, in the unlikely event, he gets this far.'

Mrs Dexter turned off the A12 at the Crown interchange and pulled up at the entrance to a hotel. "You don't have to kill me," she said.

'…schools and work places have been placed in lockdown and residents told that anybody walking the streets is in danger of being arrested as the hunt for the killer continues…'

"I'm not going to kill you!" I collected the Uzis and my jacket. "Thanks for the lift," and climbed from the car. As I walked away I heard her shout good luck... I didn't look back.

Chapter 40

Whatever the guy was saying on the radio about total lockdown in Colchester, there was still loads of traffic about. As I walked past a factory at the beginning of Ipswich Road, I noticed a police checkpoint had been set up at Severalls Lane. It would have been too suspicious for me to turn-about and walk in the direction I'd just come from. I stopped to think. Wearing my jacket, to hide the guns, with the hood up, to hide my face, on such a warm day looked weird as well.

The cops weren't stopping cars and searching them, just looking inside as they drove past slowly. I could see they were trying to scare people, the way they glared. Fucking cops! As far as I'm concerned, they'll never change, we'd all be better off without them.

The checkpoint was causing the traffic to build up and the cars weren't moving any faster than I could walk. I was wondering about the risk of doing an about turn when a bus stopped and the door opened... I'd been pondering at a bus stop. I climbed aboard and handed over my fare. The driver didn't even look at me. It would have been better if it had been a double-decker or if the thing had been full, but it was neither; single deck and empty.

I sat towards the back, took off the jacket and covered the Uzis with it. We sailed straight through the police cordon. There was another police check point at the roundabout at the top of Cowdray Avenue, where this time drivers were being flagged down and spoken to, but the bus turned towards the town centre and was waved on by a stupid constable.

There was more police activity. Sirens howled and the sound of helicopters flew overhead. Three police cars and one police mini bus raced past the bus. I got off just past East Gates, where the edge of the park met the road, and walked alongside the river towards home.

Considering what I must have looked like; hood up and dirty, I was amazed I wasn't stopped. Even though here were no police in that area of the park, you could bet your life on some dip-stick who'd want to have a go. I was beginning to feel that luck was on my side. Home! I know I said that I wasn't ever going back but I needed to get cleaned up. Maybe Emma was there. If she was it would be a good and bad thing at the same time… how the hell do I tell her about Dais! And how the hell don't I tell her about Dais…

*   *   *

I didn't want all this. It had all got totally out of hand. If I'd gone to the police when Deer had done me perhaps none of this would have happened, perhaps they'd have found Josh by now as well. Maybe Dais would still be alive, even if she was heading for some Arab's harem. At the same time, if the cops weren't bent perhaps Deer would have been banged up a long time ago, so it was as much their fault. My duck make-up was stinging my eyes as the sweat caused it to run. It was a good job there wasn't anybody about to see the state I was in. I wondered where the gang was… or Fallon.

I made it to my street without any hassle and found the house quiet. I let myself in and quickly checked the place. Emma's and Dais' stuff was still piled up in the middle of the back bedroom, and Stick's in the corner. But, no Emma. I ran the bath. I nicked some of the girls' soap, washed myself and my jeans and socks and pants, drained the dirty water and filled the bath again. This time I climbed in without wearing anything and laid back and soaked.

All of a sudden blue flashing lights streaked through the window as cop cars pulled up outside on the street, quickly followed by a hell of a crash. Somebody smashed through the front door. This was it! I was resigned to being caught. Maybe it would be for the best, and I waited for the bathroom door to fly open. Heavy footsteps climbed the stairs and stamped through the bedrooms. I tensed up. "Clear up here," shouted a voice, and the footsteps returned down to the ground floor. I couldn't make out much of what was being said as voices from mouths shouted and voices from radios crackled, but there was a lot of activity.

"I want an officer present," a voice commanded. "This is a crime scene and I don't want anybody contaminating it, under any circumstances, until forensics get here."

And there I was, laying in the bath, Uzis up against the wall, trapped. I took my time and finished soaking, and after that I quietly rubbed down my jacket and squeezed as much water out of my jeans as I could. I slipped part way down the stairs. The front door had been closed, although I could see it had been smashed. When I sneaked a look through the bedroom windows the place was surrounded by blue and white tape and an armed cop wearing flack-jacket and high-viz stood on duty at the front. I hoped he melted in this heat. I almost let the water out of the bath, without thinking. I hung my dirty shirt across the toilet pan and placed a pair of Emma's shoes, one on each tap, to remind me not to flush the loo or drain any water away.

I knew I could jump from the back bedroom window onto the shed roof if it came to it, I'd done it before. So I had everything ready, just in case, and hung my wet jeans from the centre light… and waited.

Time dragged. I was hyped up with everything that had happened, and the cops outside. I could hear loads of activity and sneaked a few looks through the windows. Cops were going door to door, interviewing people and searching gardens. Until forensics got here, this was the safest place for me to be. I remembered that we could climb into next door's house from our loft, so I climbed up there to see if it was still the case. It was. But not only that, when Farthin's blokes had nicked everything, they'd missed the attic. It was stuffed full of old stuff... including an old radio!

I tuned into Radio Colchester. They were blaming me for killing Deer and Pete the Sleaze, which I guessed they would, eventually, but they'd found Stick's body, and they were saying *that* was probably me as well. A police spokesman said there was no proof, yet, that I did it, but I was probably the most dangerous killer ever to roam the streets of our country and on no account should I be approached. If you see me, phone 999. Check the television to see what I looked like. Fuck!

I was doing alright, with the house quarantined and the police making sure nobody got in to contaminate it, but soon I'd have to go out to get something to eat. I needed a disguise. I searched through the attic, through bags of Rosie's old clothes, maybe there was a wig or something, but I wasn't that lucky. I found a pair of sunglasses; pink. Dad had some stuff as well and there was a bag of old fashioned shirts. Putting one of those on made me look different. That would have to do. I put trousers, shirt and proper shoes on, added the glasses, hid the guns under the girls' clothes in the middle of the bedroom floor and slipped out the back door.

I wanted to eat so I don't know what made me think of it, today was the inter-house sports day at school. Our school has four 'Houses' and, obviously, I was in 'Castle House', all the gang were. Everybody is put in a House when they started at Saint Hel's, and that's where you stayed… normally. I started in *Priory House*.

I was getting terrible headaches, so bad they were making me mad, and when the doctor couldn't figure out what was causing them I suggested that I should be moved into *Castle House*, which, eventually, I was… and I've never had a headache since. For about a term anybody could go to their head of year and say they felt a bad head coming on, could they move to *Castle*… and they did! So the whole gang ended up together.

Castle House wins everything except chess. I think we're the best, but, at the same time, if we lose, people tend to get beat up.

So. Sports Day. I felt an urge to find out how we were getting on. I walked to the Avenue of Remembrance, where you could see the entire school playing fields. Dirty old men often gawped from there; until the cops were called. The grassy edge of the road sloped down to the fenced school perimeter, an ideal place to sit and observe, which is exactly what I did.

The playground was packed with kids. So much for *the entire shut down of Colchester*. I made myself comfortable against a fat tree-trunk and it wasn't long before I began to regret my decision to leave school. I could see Lee and Spider getting warmed up for the four hundred metres race. I scanned the whole sports field for Fallon and Mo and Fran but I couldn't see any of them. I also couldn't see the master score board. I bet *Castle* was well ahead though.

The area around the start and finishing lines were buzzing with teachers, kids and volunteer helpers, the sun was shining… and I felt as though I'd been cheated out of something special. I should be in school, not marauding around the countryside being England's most wanted criminal… ever!

Lee and Spider weren't in the first four hundred and the kid representing *Castle* only went and came fucking last! He was so slow that the others would have had to walk backwards to let him win. The two were in the next race though. The back straight was only about fifty metres away from me. As the starting pistol sounded and they raced round the bend I forgot I was the most wanted and most dangerous person this country had ever had and started to jump up and down and shout and holler encouragement.

Lee was in the lead and saw me. I laughed and waved. He fucking stopped and shouted… "Bloody hell… THE GAY AVENGER!" and left the running track and scampered screaming towards the school building.

At first the others were bewildered. All the racers stopped in astonishment, but as soon as they realised who I was they followed him, screaming in terror. Within seconds all the kids, the parents and the teachers were fighting each other to escape from me, clambering to get into the school block, off the field. Some kids were rescued by their volunteer mothers, but many others were left on the grass after being trampled in the stampede... left to the mercy of the Gay Avenger. I was rooted to the spot in disbelief.

The sound of approaching sirens pulled me from my shock. I ran towards Cowdray Avenue and slipped into a side street only moments before cop cars screeched past. I needed to get back to the house... fast. I took off the stupid pink sunglasses, pulled up the collar of the shirt and walked slowly with my head down, but watching everything at the same time. I got to the other side of the main street at Middleborough by going under the river bridge and that way made it to the back streets of home.

Before going to the house I went to Fallon's place and broke into their shed. In a secret tin I knew she used I found Stick's gun, the ammo and the cash. All around in the distance police cars wailed and helicopters screamed. Going to the school was a really stupid thing to do... and I was still hungry.

And I was angry with Lee, the fucking idiot. So much for mates! I took off the stupid old man's clothes and put on my gear. I found a sweat shirt amongst Dais' stuff and put it on. I could smell her... reminded me what I had to do. I slung the Uzis over my shoulders then my jacket over them. I knew I stood out in this heat but I couldn't give a fuck any more. If the fucking cops try and stop me… I'll shoot them!

I made my way up North Hill to the chippie…

Chapter 41

"Hey mate, you have to put your hood down if you want to be served in here." The bloke behind the counter.

All I wanted was a bag of chips... I ignored him. I couldn't see what the problem was anyway, there was only me and him and another bloke frying. My picture flashed across the screen of the telly and I tried to listen to what was being said.

The bloke behind the counter had another go, "Mate..."

"Shhhh..."

"*We have a message for the Gay Avenger.*" I was all ears... and suddenly Josh appeared. Josh. My little brother! I couldn't believe it... Josh, alive... not dead, not kidnapped, but there, on the telly, sitting next to some fucking woman.

"*If you're watching this broadcast Jacob Manners, listen to your brother. Go ahead Josh...*"

"*Hello, Jake. If you're watching this, give yourself up. Don't kill anybody else. You can come and live with us, me and our real mum, she's nice. Please, please Jake, please take care.*"

The woman said some words but I was so concentrating on my little brother's face that I didn't hear anything she had to say. Then the penny dropped... the woman was my mum!

The bloke stepped out from behind the counter. Instinctively I pulled out Stick's gun and pointed it straight at him, without taking my eyes off the screen.

"Chips!"

Like lightning he returned to his spot and quickly started to sort out a bag... he didn't even ask me anything, like, if I wanted them wrapped, and stuff, you know.

"And a battered sausage." I was dizzy, confused. What was Josh doing on the telly? He should be chained up somewhere, at least. And who was he with? Our real mum! Our real fucking mum! "Give me a coke as well." If he was with *our* mum... where did the money come from? Why was it shoved through our door? Slowly it dawned on me. Our real mum had paid Dad for Josh... And I was jealous...she didn't want me, she just paid for Josh. All this trouble because my fucking real mum doesn't fucking want me! Dais... Stick... all the others... I shoved the gun back into my pocket, threw the wad of cash over the counter and grabbed the coke and the sausage and chips. Two and a half grand for a bag of chips!

And, what's more, most of those chips ended up on the floor anyway as I ran towards Charlie Farthin's. I did manage all the sausage though.

I couldn't think straight… everything was a blur… I headed for the club. I was making good progress, no cops in sight… until I rounded the corner close to the entrance. A squad car roared up behind me and screeched to a halt. "HEY, JACOB MANNERS. STOP!"

I pulled out Stick's gun and waved it about, stopping them dead in their tracks. It gave me enough time to make it to the club door. It was locked.

"JACOB MANNERS… DROP THE GUN… PLACE YOUR HANDS ON YOUR HEAD AND STEP FORWARD."

Suddenly the door opened and a smiling Dek pulled me in. "Looks as though you could do with some help."

"Thanks." But I didn't have time for pleasantries, "Where's Farthin and Gilbert?"

He flicked his head, "In the bar."

I was in a hurry to get to them, but he grabbed my arm, trying to hold me back. "Don't do it Jake… they'll murder you."

I slipped off my jacket and took both Uzis in my hands and, ignoring his warning, continued along the short corridor into reception. A boy at the cloakroom screamed and ran into the bar. By the time I got there, Charlie and Gilbert were on their feet, waiting.

"Hello boy," greeted Charlie, "come to visit us have you."

As he said it, both men stepped sideways, leaving a gap between them, but I had two Uzis, one trained on each of them. Charlie's hands were hanging by his side, and empty, but Gilbert had his in his pockets. I guessed there was a gun in there as well… I watched him like a hawk.

Both blokes were cocky, un-scared. Charlie was even smiling… didn't they know who they were dealing with?

"What yer plannin yer little fucker?" asked Gilbert.

"I'm gonna kill ya, both," I screamed, "for what you did to Stick, an' Dais an' all the others." I thought about Josh.

"See," said Gilbert, "Thing is, if yer was serious, bout killin us, you'd have done it straight away, when yer come into the room. What I think yer should do now is put them fuckin things down, an' then we can talk."

"Not fuckin likely, you'll kill me."

"No we won't, promise," added Charlie. "Especially as the place is surrounded by cops."

Lying fucker. I came here to get revenge, and I needed to get on with it. As I was thinking this, Gilbert stepped forward. I squeezed the trigger of the Uzi pointing at him… nothing happened, not even a click. He laughed. I swung the other one round, but that didn't fire either.

"Well, well, well." Gilbert pulled out his gun, slowly and deliberately. He shook his head slowly, "Sorry kid." There was a sharp crack… and *he* fell down.

Behind him stood Homeless, gun in hand. Charlie, moving quick for a fat bloke, turned and lunged towards the shooter… another loud crack.

What the hell was going on? Charlie and Gilbert were on the floor, writhing and moaning, and now fucking Homeless turns out to be a maniac as well, and on the rampage. Was I next? I legged it through the kitchens and left through the other door, the workers' entrance. I heard Homeless shouting after me… "STOP!" No Fucking Way!

I didn't know where I was going, and like I always seem to do when I'm troubled, I instinctively made for the park. Cops were congregating all around. Those I could see were armed and many had dogs, but they didn't try to stop me, other than shouting through their loud hailers. They kept their distance and moved at the same pace as I was moving, not very quickly.

I didn't know what to do! I felt tears well up as I thought of Josh… All those who had died, because my mum rejected me. I hadn't wanted any of this, I just thought that I was doing the right thing… All I ever wanted was to be liked. I hoped that Gilbert and Charlie were in agony, and sorry!

A helicopter flew loudly overhead and another landed on the lower park. They were trying to cut me off.

Perhaps they were waiting until I reached the open space where they could shoot me without the possibility of hitting anyone else. Whatever their game, I was ahead of them. I got through the first gate, then past the boating lake. I could see coppers making for the gate into the upper park. I wanted to get there before they did.

As I ran, something heavy hit my face. It was Dais' St Christopher… she was sending me a message… that she was looking out for me. Now I knew that I was going to be alright. "I love you Dais," kissed the necklace and waved towards heaven.

I still had the Uzis, for what they were worth! Perhaps that was why they weren't trying to stop me, they thought I would shoot them. Why didn't they work? I was sure I'd loaded them properly. As I reached the gate way I squeezed the trigger of one, and the noise frightened the life out of me. Dust and stones flew up all over the place as bullets ricocheted into the air and the gun twisted around, like it had a life of its own. Fuck! It worked!

Who's the boss now! I turned to face the fuckers. Come and get me… if you dare? An order was shouted through loud speakers… I pointed the Uzi… and fired.

There were a couple of bursts of gunfire, and then everything went quiet. I backed off through to the upper park… I couldn't believe my eyes… I could see the cops, they were there, waiting on the grassy slopes

305

on each side of the path, wearing their shitty flack jackets and armed with bigger guns than my Uzis. But all around them were thousands and thousands of kids!

I stood, in awe. I recognised lots of them, from Saint Hels, but there were more than one school's worth, definitely. As I looked around, they began to clap. They shouted. They shouted my name… "Go for it Jake." I was confused. The shouting got louder, and they started to chant, "Jacob… Jacob… Jacob…"

Maybe I should wave. I raised an arm, and an amazing cheer erupted. "Jacob… Jacob… Jacob…" I laughed. They were cheering for me. FOR ME!

Old Bob stepped out in front of me and waved me through. I laughed. "How's yer grass Bob?"

"The fastest. Use it Jake. Use it… and climb the hill."

The path looked longer than usual as it wound up to the top gates. It seemed to be getting dark, I didn't realise it was that late, and I couldn't see the top. As I put one foot in front of the other the cheering continued, louder and louder.

Lights flashed across the sky and all the faces were lit up, somebody was firing rockets.

Jeff, the horny red devil, was at the first bend, conducting the crowd with his wand… "Jacob… Jacob… Jacob…" as his other hand shot into the air, chucking up objects, where they burst into bright light. I waved to him… and he disappeared in a massive flash. When the smoke lifted he was gone, except for his little plastic bowl. I gently placed a coin in it… and puff, he was back. It was his latest and cleverest trick and I hope he could see how impressed I was. He winked and waved and laughed as I passed.

Thousands and thousands of kids squeezed onto the hill sides, all chanting. The noise was deafening… "Jacob… Jacob… Jacob…" There was so much sound I could no longer hear the cops or their helicopters. As I climbed I felt myself getting weaker and weaker… only their chanting kept me going.

I could now see the top gates. Waiting there were Fallon and Mo and the gang… and Emma, and Josh, all beckoning me, urging me on, they'd got a surprise for me, waiting, I knew the way they worked. And, you know, they had! Out stepped Dais, followed by Stick.

It was like a dream… all so unreal… I tried to remember what had happened. Everything was fading. Like dreams… you remember parts as you wake, then you don't even remember the dream!

I turned and faced the crowd, waved… and they all waved back amidst a huge roar.

As I got closer to the gate Stick stepped forward and opened his arms to greet me. All the time the chanting continued and tears of joy gushed down my cheeks.

"Me man, me man," said Stick, and the others clapped me in and crowded around me. "Me prodigy music man," continued Stick, and he stepped forward and wrapped his arms around me. "I love ya man, we all love ya." He was squeezing so tightly I began to black out… but I was so happy I didn't care… and to think I thought I wasn't loved! Right at that moment I was happier than I'd ever been in my whole life.

Homeless got to the bottom gate, too late, and sunk to his knees. He flashed his warrant card, halting the closest flak jacket wearing policeman.

After a short period, he stood and faced the approaching hordes of policemen. He held up a small black book, prodding it as he screamed above the roar of helicopters and wails of sirens… "In here are the names of every copper on Farthing's payroll… bent coppers who helped kill this boy…" Tears born from anger streamed down his face as he scanned the dark blue mass, daring any to challenge him. "I'll be coming for each and every fucking one of you. Now, all of you… stand back… do not approach this child."

He turned and fell to his knees again, alongside the crumpled and bloody body. He stroked the kid's hair and whispered, "I'm so sorry Jacob Manners."

I try to imagine that being dead is like being alive, but… there are no people… Fuckin' People!

The End

Printed in Great Britain
by Amazon